Even as Kenyatta stared out of the window, dumbfounded, flames surrounded the police car and in seconds it was a ball of fire.

"We're goin' to have to go through it to get out, man," Kenyatta said as he searched for the safest route out of the flaming death.

"Go on through the motherfucker then," Jug ordered harshly from the back of the car. "We don't stand a chance if we keep sittin' here!"

"We don't stand a chance if I drive straight through that wall of flame either," Kenyatta yelled back. Suddenly he spotted a small chance for them. The garage door was open and it led toward the rear of the garage, which was wide open. So far the flames hadn't moved over and consumed the building.

With a vicious twist of the wheel, Kenyatta swung the car around in a quick turn and drove straight toward the door. Even as the big car picked up speed, a line of fire was leaping toward their only means of escape.

"Oh sweet motherfucker!" Peggy prayed. "Don't let it end like this! Please Lord."

Kenyatta gritted his teeth and stomped down on the gas pedal.

Holloway House Originals by Donald Goines

KENYATTA'S ESCAPE

DONALD GOINES

Kensington Publishing Corp.
http://www.kensingtonbooks.com

HOLLOWAY HOUSE CLASSICS are published by

Kensington Publishing Corp.
119 West 40th Street
New York, NY 10018

All Kensington Titles, Imprints, and Distributed Lines are
available at special quantity discounts for bulk purchases
for sales promotions, premiums, fund-raising, and educa-
tional or institutional use. Special book excerpts or cus-
tomized printings can also be created to fit specific
needs. For details, write or phone the office of the Kensington special sales manager: Kensington Publishing
Corp., 119 West 40th Street, New York, NY 10018, attn:
Special Sales Department, Phone: 1-800-221-2647.

HOLLOWAY HOUSE Reg. U.S. Pat. & TM Off.

ISBN-13: 978-0-7582-8744-1
ISBN-10: 0-7582-8744-5

First Kensington trade paperback printing: May 2013

10 9 8 7 6 5 4 3 2 1

Printed in the United States of America

DEDICATED TO

Ron and his lady Barbara. Hope they continue to keep gettin' big money. Also, I'd like to mention Jim-Jim, a young man who has the talent to write but won't take the time to develop it. Last but not completely forgotten is Linda, for what could have been, had it not been for her schizophrenic reprehension. Yet even this affirmation or pertinacious manifestation could have been coped with, but never could I accept her perpetual indulgence in extreme frugality.

1

THE POLICE LEFT Kenyatta's club on the north side of Detroit and headed toward Kenyatta's farm in the country. Some of the people there were making hurried efforts to leave. As soon as the club had been raided, Kenyatta had been called and duly informed. The few members inside the club hadn't stood up too long before giving out the information on Kenyatta's whereabouts. Kenyatta had expected just that. The members left at the club were occasional members and were not of the caliber of the hard-core members who made up the main part of the organization.

Kenyatta had every reason to be moving fast. For some time he had been actively working on two dream projects. First, he wanted to knock off every honkie cop who had it in for Blacks. And the attacks had been smoothly calculated and swift.

Many a cop had never known what had ripped his guts open before the concrete came up to meet his face.

The second project was to rid the ghetto of all the junk pushers. The slick ones who drove the big hogs, who sometimes only fronted for the big men. Big men like Kingfisher, who sat up in a cool penthouse and raked in the money. Nickels and dimes turning into thousands of dollars. Black dollars!

And so Kenyatta had Kingfisher hit. And the word was out.

The four males who left the farm with Kenyatta were all armed to the teeth. Even the women who escorted the men were strapped down with deadly weapons. Jug and his girlfriend Almeta both carried a brace of .38 specials, while Eddie-Bee and his lady favored .44 magnums. Red and Arlene each carried sawed-off shotguns.

Kenyatta and Betty, with over thirty thousand dollars in a black briefcase, rode with Zeke and his Black queen. The couples piled into waiting cars in the farmyard and made haste to leave before the police arrived.

The rest of the people watched them go, not knowing when the leader would return to the farm. Ali, Kenyatta's brother, stood at the front door scratching his chin. He had been left in charge and that was almost all that mattered to him. The tall brown-skinned bald-headed man felt uneasy. But he couldn't put his finger on it. There was no way for him to know that his rule would last but a few hours.

Ali didn't have the knowledge that Kenyatta possessed. He was uninformed about the raid on the city clubhouse, and he didn't know that an army of police were on their way out to the gang's hide-out at the farm at that moment. So he stood on the front porch and swelled his chest, breathing the clean country air, daydreaming about how sweet the future would be if something happened to Kenyatta. He figured, he'd have no problem stepping into Kenyatta's shoes and taking over the smooth-running organization. Ali looked over the farm buildings. The well-kept cabins with their freshly painted doorways. Everywhere he looked he saw young Black couples, dedicated men and women who believed in their cause.

The drive to the airport was swift. Before Kenyatta could finish smoking his second cigarette they were turning into the lane that led to the terminal. When they reached the busy terminal Kenyatta and his followers parked their cars in a no-standing zone. There was no thought of returning to the automobiles. It was time to get out. In the last short minutes at the farm Kenyatta had briefed his small group again on their plan of escape. It was well thought out and they had been over and over it in practice runs in the past. Now it was time to put it to use.

Everybody followed Kenyatta into the airport. As he bypassed the ticket windows he turned and joked with his followers. "Now that sure in the hell would be a waste of good money, wouldn't it?" He shifted the heavy black bag containing the money around to his left hand.

All of the Black women carried large shoulder bags. Each couple had a certain amount of cash on them in case they ran into more trouble than they could handle and had to split. But none of them carried as much as Kenyatta did.

They waited about ten minutes until the regular passengers began boarding a nonstop flight to California. Kenyatta led his small dedicated group toward the loading ramp. The airport was set up in such a way that they didn't check for weapons until the passengers were going toward the ramp that led to the plane. Then you had to pass through a small space where they had a metal detector. Near the detector, a few guards stood around, looking bored, as they watched the metal detector to see if anyone was carrying a weapon.

When Kenyatta's group reached the guards, there was no suspicion. Kenyatta's group was well dressed and smiling. They came toward the detector slowly, acting as if they owned tickets, then suddenly all hell broke loose. Kenyatta pulled out an automatic. He waved it at the group of guards as his people came rushing up beside him. With a wave of his hand, Red went rushing up the ramp.

The sight of the Black men trying to commandeer the plane sent the guards into action. As Red came rushing past, one of the guards tried to reach out and detain him with his outstretched arm while another took a step back and pulled out his .38 police special from his shoulder holster. Neither man found success. The first guard took a bullet from Red's gun in the face. Blood flew everywhere as the white guard crumpled in a heap on the floor. His face had been replaced by a red gash. The young, attractive stewardess who had been standing nearby screamed loudly as she stared, horrified, at the dead man.

As the second guard came out with his gun Red's woman Arlene, who was just a step behind her man, shot from the hip and took the guard by surprise. His first shot hit him high, the heavy slug smashing him viciously in the chest and spinning him around. The second shot took the back of the man's head off. The couple ran past, not bothering to take a second look as the object of their handiwork fell to the ground.

"Everybody stay still," Kenyatta ordered loudly, "and won't nobody get hurt." As he spoke a guard on Kenyatta's blind side made his move. As soon as the man reached for his weapon, Betty stepped around her man and raised the sawed-off shotgun she carried in her bag. The gun was cut so short that it was almost the same size as a pistol. She gave the guard both barrels. The shotgun kicked back in her hands so hard she damn near dropped the weapon. Both barrels at short range tore the man on the receiving end to pieces. His stomach and chest dissolved before the very eyes of the other watching men. Blood and guts flew everywhere.

The sight of what the shotgun did froze the other guards in their tracks. Fear was written all over their faces. There was no doubt in their minds now as to whether or not the Blacks meant business.

Kenyatta backed up the ramp after taking the girl who had worked at the checkpoint as his shield. He stopped and waved Betty and the rest of his crowd past. They rushed up the ramp toward Red, who had the stewardess shaking from fear at the sight of his pistol.

Kenyatta's measured words roared out over the airport. "You honkies had better pay heed, or we'll kill everything white on the plane!" A dark flush stained his lean and shallow cheeks as rage glittered in his cold black eyes.

The sight of the terrified white girl in the tall Black man's arms made the guards hesitate. There was no doubt that he'd kill her. The guards held their weapons in check and allowed the wild-eyed Kenyatta to make his way on up the ramp.

Eddie-Bee stood at the top of the ramp waiting for him. He pointed two .38 short-nosed police specials at the white men standing at the bottom of the ramp.

"That's right," Kenyatta roared as he backed into the airplane, followed closely by Eddie-Bee. "If you don't want any dead passengers or stewardesses, keep your hands off them motherfuckin' guns!" His voice carried all the way through the plane, causing a near panic among the already frightened passengers.

The members of his gang had already taken complete command of the airplane. The pilot was well aware of the fact that his plane had been commandeered by a bunch of Black gunmen. He reached the tower by radio and asked for information on what to do.

"Follow their orders. Don't endanger any of the passengers' lives," the voice from the tower replied. "The people who have taken control of your plane are murderers. They have just killed at least four people that we know of in the terminal. For Christ's sake, be careful!"

The co-pilot glanced over at his captain and their eyes locked for a quiet moment. But that was broken by Zeke's sudden entrance. The tall Black man stood in the cockpit with a cocked gun in his hand.

He aimed it at the back of the co-pilot's head. "It won't be any trouble if you don't give us any," the Black man stated harshly.

From the way the man had spoken, the pilots knew he meant business. "Where to?" the captain inquired softly.

"When we get off the ground I'll personally let you know," Zeke replied, then smiled. It had gone easier than Kenyatta had said it would. "Wherever we go," Zeke said offhandedly, "you can bet it will be where a Black man is treated like a man. Yes indeed!" Zeke was speaking more to himself than to the white pilots. "It's goin' sure 'nuff be where a Black man can be a man!"

2

KENYATTA STOOD AT the open hatch of the airplane until the men removed the ramp. The airplane was ready now to take off. As the door closed he walked slowly up the aisle, his sharp glance taking in the way his members had everything under control. All of the passengers were sitting quietly in their seats, watching the proceedings out of fear-ridden eyes. Most of them were looking for the sudden arrival of the police, but as the jet engines started up, this hope died quickly. The sound of the jets roaring shattered the hopes of just about all the passengers. Now, they had only to look forward to a deadly ride to God knew where. Each passenger huddled in his seat, wondering wildly where it would all end. As Kenyatta walked past, most of them glanced down at the floor, afraid to look him directly in the eye.

Sitting in the rear of the airplane, private guard James Carson tried to catch the eye of Will Coney, a flight marshal hired by the airlines. When Carson finally managed to catch Coney's attention, the marshal held up a finger for patience. Carson settled back in his seat and began to put his seatbelt on. The pilot's voice came over the speaker informing all the passengers to do the same.

As soon as Kenyatta heard the pilot's voice, he walked to the back of the plane and motioned to the fat white man sitting in the last seat by himself. "Okay, honkie," Kenyatta ordered sharply, "you better get up front and find you another seat." Kenyatta stared at the white man closely. For a second he didn't believe the white was going to do as he said. He had just about decided to blow the man's brains out when the fat man got up slowly from his seat and started up the aisle.

Kenyatta stared after the middle-aged white man. He could read the dislike in the man's eyes, but there was something else there that he hadn't been able to read. At that moment he decided to take a closer look at the honkie later on. For the moment, though, Kenyatta settled down in the seat. Betty came rushing from the front of the airplane and joined him, just as the pilot warned everybody again to fasten their seatbelts.

Private guard James Carson settled down in the seat beside Detective Will Coney. "Goddamn it," Will cursed under his breath, "why didn't you pick another seat somewhere? We don't want these jigs to get suspicious of us."

"It's all right," James assured him. "That tall nigger made me move out of my rear seat, so he don't suspect nothing."

Will let out a sigh. "I hope the hell you know what you're talkin' about, Carson, because these niggers are playing for keeps."

"I believe we can take them, Will," Carson stated, his voice revealing more than anything else his urge for action.

"Take hell," Will replied. "Are you out of your fuckin' skull? Listen, Carson, don't start no hero shit on this trip, because we're outnumbered and don't stand a chance in hell of takin' all these jigs by surprise! So don't get no fuckin' ideas that might get some innocent passengers killed. No sir," Will continued, "we're just along for the ride on this one, unless something comes up that we can't overlook. Then maybe we'll have to toss off our cover. But not until!"

The words that Will Coney spoke went in one ear and out another. James Carson had no intention of letting such a good opportunity get past him. If he could somehow regain control of the airplane for the airline, his picture would be in every paper in the country. It was too good a chance for him to pass up. He might go a lifetime and never get another opportunity like this one. That he might lose his own life in the endeavor never entered his mind.

"Will," Carson answered, "if they start knockin' off the passengers, I don't plan on sitting on my fat ass and just watching them, I can tell you that much!"

"Yeah, Carson, let's worry about that one when we are confronted with it. So far, they haven't bothered anybody on this flight yet."

"What the hell you think all that goddamn shooting was about just a few minutes ago?" Carson demanded sharply.

"Whatever it was, it didn't concern us. Our job is to take care of the people on this airplane, Carson. Whatever went on at the terminal was up to the guards that worked there." Before Carson could say anything, Will continued. "They came aboard so fuckin' quick I didn't know what the hell was happenin' until I was staring down the barrel of a double-barreled shotgun that one of them fuckin' cunts was handling."

James Carson let out a curse and stared down angrily at the smaller man next to him. "I wish to hell I would have got a break like that with only some fuckin' broad covering me. I don't think them fuckin' women really know which end is up. Shit, Will, you should have took the fuckin' thing from her and rammed it up her fuckin cunt!"

Will laughed good-naturedly. "I didn't see you taking any weapons from anybody, Carson."

"Hell, I didn't have any woman covering me either. That little light-skinned bastard had two fuckin' pistols aimed at me before I knew what was happening!" Carson stated sharply, as he remembered the embarrassing incident.

"Well, don't worry about it," Will warned. "Maybe it's best we didn't show our hand, because there's at least eight of them that I'm sure of. Two of us can't do very much against that many odds. And you keep that in, buddy."

Carson glared at the other man but didn't make any comment. His mind was wandering. He pictured himself getting off the airplane as newspapermen fell over each other trying to reach him for an interview. The more he dreamed about it, the wilder his imagination became. He could see himself explaining it over and over again to beautiful women. Blondes, redheads. His mind held vivid pictures of movie stars . . . , all of them were now at his feet. He could see himself being cold and aloof as he told of the gun battle that he had won as he took back control of the airplane. The thought was so pleasant that for the next hour Carson sat back in his seat and just dreamed.

Kenyatta sat quietly next to Betty and spoke in glowing tones of the new world they would find when they reached their destination, Algiers. The trip so far had been so peaceful that most of the Black men and women had relaxed, quite sure that they now had the airplane well under control.

Breaking off his conversation, Kenyatta waved his hand in the air so that he could catch the attention of one of the stewardesses who were standing in the rear of the plane. As the woman approached, Kenyatta spoke to her quietly. "Why don't you and the other girls begin serving the passengers their dinners?"

The woman stared at him with frightened eyes, but the softness of his voice slowly removed most of the fear. She attempted to smile as she nodded her head in agreement. She went back and spoke to the other woman. Soon every passenger who could eat had a tray of food.

As the time slowly went past, Kenyatta glanced out the window and noticed that it was still light outside. He glanced at his watch and was surprised to see that it was past eight o'clock in the evening. An hour later he glanced at his watch again and frowned after seeing that it was still daylight.

With his temper slowly rising, he made his way up toward the front of the plane. As he walked past his friend Jug, Jug spoke up. "Anything up, brother?"

Kenyatta shrugged his shoulders. "I ain't hip, Jug, but I think the pilot is trying to play games with us."

Even though he hadn't spoken loud, his heavy voice carried through most of the airplane. Before Kenyatta had finished speaking, he was joined by Red and the smaller built Eddie-Bee.

Kenyatta smiled as the two men came up. "Hold on, brothers, it don't take all this. I just want to check out something, that's all." He waited until the two men returned to their seats before continuing on his way.

Without hesitation Kenyatta pushed his way into the cockpit. The pilots glanced up in surprise when he entered. "Maybe I made a mistake, boys," Kenyatta began, "by not introducing myself earlier. I happen to be the big bad nigger who's running this fuckin' thing, and I think somebody is trying to put shit in my game. Do you guys dig where I'm coming from?"

The two pilots glanced at each other, not understanding what the tall Black man meant. "I'm afraid we don't," the captain answered honestly.

"Why don't we try it again, then," Kenyatta said. "First of all, the time situation is fucked up and when I say fucked up, I mean just that. Now, by my motherfuckin' watch, it's nine-thirty in the evening. And any goddamn country boy can tell you that at that time of the evening it should be more than dusk outside." Kenyatta pointed out the window. "But when I look out like now, for instance, it ain't even that. So I got to wonderin' just what the fuck is going on. I know you been told that our destination is Algiers, so why the fuck is this time element shit coming up?"

The two pilots glanced at each other nervously before the captain replied. They had discussed the matter between themselves earlier so they came out with their prepared lie immediately. "We are nearing the West Coast. We will have to land to take on fuel in California. So the reason you still see daylight is because of the difference. You will have to set your watch back three hours if you want it to be correct now."

As the captain spoke, Kenyatta stared into the white man's eyes trying to tell if he was lying. He didn't know if they should land in California or Cuba to take on fuel. It was something he should have been aware of, but he wasn't. He could only hope that the pilot spoke the truth.

"Listen buddy," Kenyatta said, still keeping his voice low, "I'm not going to warn you again because we are not playing games. If I find out you're fuckin' around, I'm going to blow your shit out, you understand?"

He stared first at the pilot, then he glared at the copilot, so that neither man really knew who the warning was for. Though neither man knew for sure, they each felt that the Black man meant every word he said. There was something about the tall man that made them respect his words. They watched as he turned his back on them and left the cockpit.

When the co-pilot reached for the radio, the captain brushed his hand away. "No," he warned, "we have followed orders and have flown toward California so that they will be ready when we land in Los Angeles. There's no reason for us to take any more chances than we have al. . . ."

That was as far as the captain got. The door opened quietly and Kenyatta stood in the doorway. As the two white men glanced around, the first thing they noticed was that this time he wasn't empty-handed.

The pistol seemed to grow larger and larger as the two men stared into the short barrel of the snub-nosed .38. The clean-headed Black man seemed to be smiling as he raised the gun. At the last minute, the copilot realized that the gun was pointed in his direction. He started to rise from his seat when the first gunshot exploded in the tiny compartment. The concussion from the gun almost broke their eardrums.

The bullet caught the co-pilot in the side of his forehead and came out of the other side of his head. Brains and blood splattered the windshield. As his co-pilot fell against the paneling the captain stared in shocked horror. He couldn't believe what he saw. The fact that his friend had been killed in cold blood was too much for him to accept. His eyes bugged outward and for a minute his face paled so much that it seemed as if he was having a stroke.

Without hesitating, Kenyatta raised the gun and aimed it at the captain. "If I have to, man, you'll be next." From the look in his eyes the captain believed every word the Black man had spoken.

Before the captain could get himself completely under control, all hell broke loose in the rear of the airplane. The two men in the cockpit could only stare behind them, dumbfounded.

The sounds of gunfire coming from the cockpit

set the stage for violence. At the first gunshot most of the Black men rushed toward the front of the plane. As they gathered in front of the thin doorway, undecided on whether or not to break in, they appeared to be very vulnerable.

At the sight of the men standing there confused, Carson saw an answer to his dreams. Here was the wonderful opportunity that he had prayed for. There was no doubt in his mind whether or not they could take the confused men. The women didn't disturb him whatsoever, because he was sure that they would just toss their guns down once things began to get hot. He didn't even bother to consult Will Coney.

Reaching under his arm, Carson drew out his pistol and opened fire. At the first sight of the gun in Carson's hand, Will cursed under his breath. He didn't bother to argue because it was too late. Carson was committing them to a lopsided gunfight that couldn't have but one ending.

Will was a man who faced life without any false beliefs. What was white was white, what was black was black. It was as clear as that. Now, as he pulled out his gun, he knew that death was the only thing that they would get out of the gunfight. The odds were too long, it was impossible for them to win.

The passengers inside the plane began to scream. Most of them were white. Three Black women traveled with a Black man and, at the sight of the guns in the white men's hands, the Black man tried desperately to get the three women to lie down out of the way.

The first shot from Carson's gun took the tall dark-complexioned Zeke in the back. He had been standing at the rear of the crowd of Black men, waiting to find out what was happening inside the cockpit. The impact of the bullet knocked him into two of the other men.

Before they could react to the sudden ambush, another shot rang out and this time the short husky Red was hit. He spun around from the shock of the slug but managed to stay on his feet. The bullet had struck him high in the left shoulder. As Carson drew down on the bewildered bunch of men again, the Black women went into action.

Zeke's woman Ann let out a scream of rage as she saw her man go down. It took a moment for her to find out where the gunshot came from. In her rage and hurt she had first started to run up the aisle toward the stricken man. Then, at the sight of the two white men with guns in their hands, she tried to pull up. Her sawed-off shotgun was just coming up when Will took careful aim and shot her in the chest. The force of the bullet knocked the tall brown-skinned woman off her feet and on top of a white woman passenger.

Betty, using the same cold, deadly concentration that her man Kenyatta used, fired slowly from the hip with the short .44 magnum she carried. The bullet took Will an inch over the heart, killing him instantly.

The sounds of the gunshots and screams of the frightened passengers caused bedlam on the large airplane. One woman passenger jumped up from her seat, screaming in panic, and began to run wildly up the aisle. The Black men at the front of the plane now stood with their backs to the cockpit as they searched frantically for their ambusher. The sight of the screaming woman was too much for one of them. Eddie-Bee couldn't control his reflexes. After throwing down the fleeing woman, his trigger finger finished what he hadn't meant to do. He squeezed off a shot, taking the woman in the back. She staggered from the blow, then continued to run until one of the Black women raised a gun and put her out of her misery. The bullet took the woman in the forehead.

Carson was still on his feet. Somehow he had managed to escape being hit. As he raised his gun again, it dawned on him that he was fighting a losing battle. The sight of his dead companion beside him brought home the truth of the matter. Now there were no more daydreams. What Will had tried to warn him about was coming true. There would be no large parades with him as the main event. The hero of the moment was only dreaming. The only thing he would get out of this was a hero's death. No beautiful women would be flocking around begging to be in his company.

Now there was only the chance of taking some of his killers with him. After he took a quick glance over his shoulder, the blood froze in his veins. The Black women he had so readily ignored were all armed, and before he could take his eyes off them, he saw at least three of them pointing weapons at him. The barrage that struck him was awesome. He was dead before ever reaching the floor.

After Carson's death, the sounds of gunfire died out. People stared around at the carnage—bodies were everywhere.

Betty leaned down and felt Ann's pulse. When she rose there were tears in her eyes. "The son-ofabitch killed her," she cursed.

Red's short brown-skinned woman, Arlene, started up the aisle toward her man, who was stretched out on the floor. As she passed the three Black passengers, one of the women started to scream at her.

"What's wrong with you folks? You ain't nothing but animals, that's all! Just goddamn animals! You all need to be dead somewhere," the woman cursed. "Just killin' people like you ain't got good sense. Makes me shame to be Black."

All at once Arlene lost her reasoning. The sight of her man lying on the floor and now this woman screaming in her face was too much. Without hesitation, Arlene raised the pistol she carried and fired pointblank at the Black woman in front of her. The force of the bullet took the woman in the breast and lifted her off her feet. She fell back amongst her friends, dead.

Arlene waved the pistol at the rest of the group of Blacks. "Now, has any more of you self-righteous motherfuckers got anything else to say?" Her eyes went from one face to the other. Each one clamped their mouth shut, knowing their life depended on silence.

As she went on past the group, Betty walked up and warned them. "Your friend brought that on herself. I hope the rest of you learned something from it. We wouldn't have hurt none of you. All you had to do was remain silent and stay the fuck out of the way. Now, one of your comrades is dead, just because she couldn't keep a lid on her mouth. Let's hope that the rest of you value your lives more than she did, because this is no game we are playing. This is for keeps, so just keep it in mind." Betty walked on toward the front of the plane. Suddenly the airplane went into a nosedive, throwing Betty off her feet. Everyone was jolted out of place as the airplane went out of control.

The sudden nosedive took Kenyatta by surprise, too. He was tossed on top of the control panels. As he fought to regain his feet, he noticed the captain bent over his controls. The man was fighting to regain the control of the airplane, but Kenyatta could tell from his actions that he was hurt. There was blood all over the back of his chair.

"Pull it out, captain," Kenyatta ordered sharply, as he struggled to get into the co-pilot's seat.

Just when it seemed as if they would never come up out of the dive, the pilot finally managed to regain some control of the plane. The plane straightened out, but the pilot was slumped over the controls.

Kenyatta glanced down at the ground below. All he could see from his seat was sand hills. "It looks as if we're over some kind of desert, captain, so if you don't think you can make it, put this motherfucker down. You hear, captain? Put this motherfucker down on the ground at once!"

The wounded pilot nodded his head, then tried to pull himself together.

"We're somewhere over the Nevada desert," the pilot managed to say. "I'm going to try and put her down somewhere. The passengers will have a better chance that way than they will with me at the controls. I don't think I can make it much longer."

"Where you hit at?" Kenyatta inquired, as he stared at the wounded man.

"In the back, boy," the captain stated as he let out a groan. "It's a bad one too."

"Okay, captain," Kenyatta said, "then it's up to you. You've got a lot of lives back there depending on you. I know if it was just me and my bunch you'd let this motherfucker fall clean out of the sky, but it ain't. You've got a hell of a lot of innocent lives on this plane that depend on you being able to land them safe."

As Kenyatta spoke, the pilot began to ease the huge airplane down out of the sky. In seconds they were inches above the desert floor. The pilot used the last of the daylight to see where he was landing.

"I just hope like hell we don't hit any sand dunes," the pilot moaned as he let the wheels touch down for the first time.

Kenyatta stared out of the window, trying to see what they were rushing toward. He couldn't make out anything because of the speed of the large airplane.

"I can't see a fuckin' thing," he yelled over to the pilot, as both men strained their eyes searching the desert floor for danger.

"That's good," the captain assured him. "If you don't see anything looming up out of the ground in front of us it means that it's smooth." Before the words were out of his mouth they hit a small ditch that almost jolted the huge plane out of the pilot's control. He fought the wheel until he had regained control, but it seemed to take the last strength out of his body. He slumped over in his seat. The plane raced across the ground at breakneck speed.

Kenyatta reached over and snatched the pilot. "Don't kick out on me now," he yelled into the captain's face. "Goddamn it, man you've got to brake this thing down, you hear me?"

Donald Goines

The pilot raised his head, then quickly pulled the controls. He hit his brakes and the airplane slowed down.

In another few seconds the huge plane rolled to a jerky stop. As the plane stopped, the pilot slumped over in his seat again. Kenyatta reached over and pulled his head back.

"Where the hell are we?" Kenyatta asked sharply. But after taking a closer look at the pilot he released the man's head. The pilot had landed the last airplane he'd ever land. He was dead. He had used his last remaining strength to land the airplane, bringing his passengers to safety for the last time.

Kenyatta stood up slowly. Well, he reflected, at least we're still alive, and as long as he had a breath in his body, he would still possess the will to survive.

3

A S SOON AS ALI was sure Kenyatta and his small
group were gone, he went into the bedroom
and began searching quietly for the large stash of
money that was kept there. He scratched his chin
as he realized that the money was gone. The tall
brown-complexioned man sat down on the edge
of the king-sized bed that took up most of the
room. He thoughtfully took out his cigarettes and
lit one. Even though he was now in charge, there
was something wrong somewhere. He couldn't
put his finger on it, but in the back of his mind he
was worried.

Where could Kenyatta have hidden the money,
he wondered over and over again. He didn't want
to accept the fact that the money was gone. That
was too much. The money didn't belong to Kenyatta
or any other single member. It was the trust fund

that they were saving for hard times, so the money had to be around somewhere. His anger was slow in coming, but gradually his temper began to boil. Just the thought of Kenyatta moving the money without telling him where it was was enough to make Ali hot. Since he was the second in charge, it was something he was supposed to know about at all times. Suppose something happened to Kenyatta, then he'd be up shit's creek if he didn't know where the trust fund was kept. Just the idea of Kenyatta's woman knowing while Ali didn't made him grit his teeth in anger.

The door of the bedroom opened and Ali's woman came in. Even though she was barely over five foot tall, she was all woman. Her hips were exceptionally large and her chest stuck out a country mile in front of her. When she smiled, a person was almost overcome by the beautiful smile she flashed, revealing teeth that movie stars would sell their souls for.

"Goddamn it," Ali cursed as she entered, "how many times have I got to tell you, Vickie, to knock on the fuckin' door before entering, okay?"

The bright smile on her face disappeared as soon as she heard his harsh words. "I'm sorry, honey," she answered, as her head dropped. "Since I knew you were in here by yourself, I didn't think it would make any difference."

"That's what's wrong with the average Black woman," Ali almost shouted at her, as his anger increased. Now that he had someone to vent his anger on, he wasn't passing up any chances. "You fuckin' women just don't think. Your brains are in your motherfuckin' cunts, right between your legs!"

Vickie blinked her eyes, fighting back the tears that were already rolling down her pretty cheeks. All of her life she had been easily hurt by what others said to her. Her feelings were more like a little girl's than a woman twenty-two years old. But no matter how hard she tried, she just couldn't control them.

Gritting his jaws tightly, Ali stared angrily at her, then added, "And just look at you. Standing there crying like a fuckin' baby. What the hell is wrong with you, Vickie? You better get hip, girl, and stop carrying your damn feelings around on your sleeve!"

"I just can't help it, Ali. I'm not used to people talking to me as if I'm a dog or something," she answered, showing more anger than she generally did.

"Bullshit!" he snorted. "If you want to get along in this fuckin' world, girl, you better learn something, 'cause soft people get stepped on every fuckin' day!"

As he stared coldly at her, his anger began to slowly disappear. It wasn't her fault, he reasoned, so why be petty and take his anger out on her? If he was honest with himself, he knew that that was just what he was doing. Since he was angry over Kenyatta rehiding the money, he was letting his anger out on his woman.

Struggling with his temper, Ali opened his arms and took her into them. The short, stocky woman stepped into them like a drowning person reaching for a life belt. Ali kissed her lips slowly at first, then as she returned his kiss with passion, he began to crush her. Because of his height, he almost had to lift her off her feet.

They were still tightly embraced when the bedroom door burst open. "Ali, Ali," the slim, dark-complexioned man in the doorway yelled. "There's motherfuckin' pigs allover the place, man! What the hell are we going to do?"

Ali released his woman quickly, then rushed out of the bedroom while Jack, the man who brought the news, followed closely on his heels. Ali rushed to the front room and snatched the curtain back. The sight of all the police cars shook him to his knees. He could feel his legs trembling. His brain raced wildly. He didn't know what to do. All the other Black men and women inside the house stared at him, waiting for him to give them some kind of order.

Ali's brain was numb, he couldn't think. He could only stand at the window and watch the white men piling out of the cars with shotguns and rifles cradled in their arms.

Detective Benson and his white partner Ryan

30

were in the second police car that pulled up in the yard. Both men began to give orders to the uniformed policemen, trying to keep things under control. Almost imperceptibly things began to slip out of the control of the two detectives.

As one uniformed officer saw three Black men run into a small white cabin, he quickly aimed the rifle he carried and took a quick shot at the fleeing men. The last man into the cabin caught the bullet in his back. He staggered inside the cabin and died on the floor. The other Black men inside the cabin had been undecided at first, but at the cold-blooded killing of their friend and companion their minds were made up for them.

Before the uniformed officer who had fired the shot could reach cover, a rifle barrel came out of the already open window and the gunman took no time aiming. His first shot took the policeman who had started the shoot-out in the forehead. The man was dead before he hit the ground. His partner let out a curse, but before he could get into action, another bullet was fired and he received the shot in his stomach.

For the first few minutes of the shoot-out the policemen were caught out in the open. Many of them were in front of their cars, not bothering to take cover because they had confidence in their numbers.

Most of the Black men and women on the farm had pulled their weapons out as soon as the first police car had pulled into the yard, so they were ready. From the various cabins gunfire erupted, taking a heavy toll on the police.

The only place gunfire wasn't coming from was from the house, where Ali had control. He was too dumbfounded at first to take any kind of action. It wasn't until some shots took the glass out of the front window pane, barely missing him, that he pulled himself together.

All at once developing rage overcame him. He came out of his lethargy with a blinding hatred for the white pigs in uniform. "Break out our shit," he ordered, but it was a useless order. Already most of the Blacks in the house were armed. Only Ali and his woman hadn't picked up weapons.

The sudden burst of gunfire from the house almost overcame the policemen. "Call for help," Ryan yelled over at a young officer in uniform. "Tell then to send reinforcements at once."

Detective Benson worked his way around to the rear of the car they had come in. He opened the trunk and removed the riot gun. Taking dead aim he began to fire slowly at the windows of the heavily occupied house.

A short Black man named Pete fell back from the wide window he had been firing out of. His face was covered with blood. As he fell to the carpet, another dedicated Black man took his place. For the next hour it was give and take. People died on both sides with more regularity than either side wanted.

Finally, a small convoy of police cars arrived. Before that, they had been coming singly and in pairs. But now there were over thirty police cars scattered over the area.

Ali took in the situation, his temper now firmly under control. He realized at once that they didn't have much of a choice. Either they continued to fight and die or they gave up and were put in prison for the rest of their lives. He had no doubts about that matter. Too many police had died in the gun battle. Somebody would have to pay for their deaths. As he studied the scene in front of him, he began to concentrate on a way out. So far, the police hadn't managed to completely surround all of the farm, because there were just too many cabins with gun-shooting Black men and women inside of them.

"Hey Dickie!" A tall, light-skinned Negro turned from a window in the dining room with all the glass blown out of it.

"What it is?" the Black man called back.

"It's time we made a move," Ali said, as he began to crawl away from his window. He kept his head down next to the floor as he carefully crawled into the dining room area.

A few of the Black people at the remaining windows stopped shooting to hear what he had to say. "Some of you keep tossing a few shots at them honkies," Ali ordered when he noticed everybody watching him.

"Listen, Dickie," he continued, "we goin' have

to make a break out of here, and it's goin' have to be soon. Them peckerwoods are going to bring up flame throwers and whatever else they need if this hit keeps up."

"I'm hip," Dickie replied. "I'm surprised they haven't brought that shit up already." He stuck his rifle barrel out the window and took a shot at an officer revealing too much of his body. He cursed when he saw the policeman jump back behind his automobile. "I should have took my time. I could have knocked that honkie off!"

Ignoring the man's words, Ali continued to crawl to the kitchen where he glanced out a window. There were too many police on that side, so he came back into the living room.

"I don't know which way we goin' make our break, but we had better come up with something damn quick," Ali stated.

"Hey Ali," a tall, dark woman called from a side bedroom. "I believe we could make it through this bedroom window. There ain't nobody really covering this side. Everybody seems to be in the front."

"I'll check it out, Ali," Jackie yelled out, then scrambled quickly into the bedroom. He was back in a minute. "She's right, Ali. The window looks out over the horses' barn. Once we make it to the barn, the damn woods ain't too far away."

"Yeah," Dickie began, then said harshly, "but what are we going to do with all our wounded? We sure in the hell can't lug them all the way to the woods. Ain't nobody goin' make it if we try and carry them along."

For the first time Ali really took a close look at the people on the floor. There were three dead bodies and that many wounded. Two of the wounded ones were women, and suddenly a dark flush stained Ali's cheeks as he noticed for the first time his woman Vickie stretched out on the floor. Blood was bubbling from a gunshot wound in her large chest, and as he crawled over to her, he could see blood on her lips.

"Oh my love," he moaned, as he cradled her in his arms. "Goddamn, goddamn," he cried over and over again. "Didn't I tell you, dumb ass woman, to stay down? Didn't I, honey?" There was no anger in his words, just the sound of a deep hurt. He held her tightly, crying openly now. "Oh, the motherfuckers," he cursed. "Goddamn it, my God, God damn it!"

After checking out the bedroom himself, Dickie crawled over to where Ali held his woman. "We got to make a move, man," Dickie stated quietly. "If we stay here much longer, there won't be no chance of nobody getting out."

Ali gestured with impatience. "Them cocksuckers done hit my woman," he stated emotionally.

"I know, man," Dickie replied quietly, "but it ain't nothing we can do about it now. It's done and we can't help Vickie out."

"That's bullshit!" Ali exploded and ran to a window, exposing himself. He snatched up a rifle and took dead aim at an officer who broke from his cover at that moment and was running for a closer car. The bullet did not kill the policeman at once. It only severed his spinal cord, paralyzing the man instantly. As he lay on the open ground screaming with pain, another policeman broke from his cover in an attempt to reach his friend and pull him to cover. Ali's first shot took the second policeman in the head, killing him instantly. A full range of bullets began to pour through the window as the angry policemen returned his deadly fire. But it was too late; Ali had dropped back to the floor and begun to crawl back toward Vickie.

When he reached her, he pulled her limp head into his lap. No one had to tell him that she was gone. No one could help her now. As he sat there holding her, Dickie went past, followed by four other people.

"It's up to you, Ali," Dickie called out. "We're on our way. If you want to stay and hold the fort down, that's cool with us."

Ali didn't even bother to glance up. It was as if he hadn't heard the words. He sat on the floor holding his dead woman in his lap. Tears of pain rained down his cheeks. He wished now that he had taken the time and told her how much he loved her. But now that he thought about it, he couldn't remember once having done it.

Suddenly his moment of sanity departed. A blind rage to kill overcame him again. All thoughts of fleeing were gone. Now only revenge remained. There was nothing else on his mind. He glanced around wildly.

Dickie stood in the door and watched him as he waited for the slower women in his small party to finish climbing out the window. At last, his young lady Peggy made it through. Without speaking again, Dickie turned his back and left. From the expression on Ali's face, Dickie knew the man was gone. He rushed to the bedroom window and stuck one leg out, then quickly climbed down. It was a short drop, only four feet from the ground.

As he landed, he could see some of the other brothers and sisters halfway to the barn, and no alarm had sounded. Dickie grabbed Peggy's arm and started running for the horse stable.

Three police officers on the far side of the large farmhouse saw the fleeing people. From behind their parked cars, they began to take aim. A young brother that everybody called Duke fell to the grass as a rifle shot took him high in the back. He let out a high-pitched yell as he rolled over. Dickie, bringing up the rear, didn't bother to look down as he roughly pulled his thin, tiny woman along. Peggy turned her head away on purpose. She had seen too many deaths that day to want to see another.

The first Black men to reach the barn, Shortman and Victor, lay down by the doorway and began to return the policemen's fire. Each man was armed with a rifle that they had brought from the farmhouse. One of the policemen pitched over, and when the other two officers glanced at their partner, they saw a gaping hole in the man's temple. The sight of their dead companion made them seek more cover. In the short breathing spell, Dickie managed to reach the horse barn. As he ran inside, he leaned back against the doorway to catch his breath. Suddenly, the sound of rapid machine gun fire came to the fleeing men and women.

After Dickie left, Ali looked around the front room, seeking a weapon. He spotted a submachine gun in the hands of a dead man. Keeping his head down, Ali made his way over to the corpse and removed the gun. As he quickly examined the bullet clip, he noticed that the man had never gotten a chance to fire the weapon. The gun was fully loaded. Using caution, Ali made his way to the nearest window. As he rose up, the first thing to come into sight were four plainclothesmen trying to "Indian" up on the side of the house. Because of the long absence of gunfire, the policemen believed everybody inside the house was dead.

Ali caught them out in the open. Two cops would run a few feet, then hit the ground, waiting until another couple repeated the same maneuver. In this way they were worming their way up to the house. At the sudden appearance of the Black man at the window, two of the plainclothesmen opened fire.

Ignoring the gunfire from the small pistols, Ali stood in full view and began to fire the automatic machine gun. In his haste, he began to spree his shots, causing him to miss all but one of the policemen. The officer that he hit was cut in half by the heavy fire from the submachine gun. The first bullets struck him in the head, then because of the rapid fire of the gun, there came a long line of bullet holes down from the back of the policeman's head to his spine.

Ryan glanced out of the corner of his eyes at his Black partner, Benson. He sighed a sigh of relief to see that his friend was still okay. Benson was lying in the grass eight feet away, holding his pistol with both hands. The Black police officer was taking dead aim. When he squeezed off his shot, the Black man standing in the window of the house, firing the submachine gun, jerked back as if he was a puppet on a string.

Ryan pulled his finger away from the trigger of his gun. As he started to stand up, the Black man in the window reappeared. With his gun pointed downward, Ryan watched the wounded man in the window raise the short-barreled sub and point it in his direction. For the first time in his life, Ryan froze. He knew that it was the end. There was no way he could raise his gun in time. The range was too short as he could see the wild-eyed gunman plainly.

The sound of an automatic went off near him and again the figure in the window was knocked backwards. Ryan glanced over and saw his partner, Benson, blowing the smoke off the barrel of his weapon, as though nothing had happened. Both men were well aware of the danger to Ryan, but neither would mention it until a much later time when they would joke about the matter.

The first bullet Ali took high in the left shoulder, and it staggered him. In seconds he had regained control of himself and had stepped back to the window. He had spotted a white man standing up—a sitting duck. He had smiled to himself as he had taken his time and aimed at the policeman. The second shot that struck Ali had taken him right in the middle of the chest. He had let out a grunt as the force of the gun shot knocked him backwards and off his feet. He hadn't realized it when the weapon he held flew from his hands. The floor striking him in the back was the final blow and the last breath in his body departed.

Had he lived, he would have seen the tractor and trailer that pulled up at about the same instant he was shot. On the back of the lowboy trailer were two army tanks.

As Benson and Ryan watched, the soldier that had driven the truck up dropped the trailer, and the tanks began to move off. Turning back to the business at hand, the two policemen finished approaching the house as the other plainclothesman came running up. The three officers tried to determine the best way to enter the house. They weren't sure that the house was empty of fighting

men. As they stood debating, four more policemen came roaring up in a squad car. The uniformed policemen jumped out before the driver
had even stopped. Now there were seven officers
of the law on the side of the farmhouse.

The uniformed officers approached the plainclothes officers and Ryan took charge at once.
"You guys give us some backup cover. We're going
right through that fuckin' front door and get this
shit over with!" Ryan stated, loudly, even though
he felt soft-spoken inside. His heart was beating
like a huge water pump that worked twenty-four
hours.

The seven policemen moved to the front of the
building. One of the uniformed officers rushed
up and kicked the door in. Before he could regain
his balance three detectives ran past him through
the front door. Their weapons were in their hands
and ready for action. The first thing that Benson
saw when he entered the front room of the farmhouse was the dead bodies lying about. A lump
came up and hung in his throat as he realized that
every dead person was Black. In less than a minute
they had searched the farmhouse and had found it
empty.

The sounds of gunfire outside brought the men
back outside.

The late evening sunlight struck Benson in his
eyes as he stepped outside. He watched the army
tanks as they moved toward the small white cabins. Under his breath he prayed for the Black men

and women to give themselves up. But even as he prayed, he knew it was useless. The policemen were now out for blood. Even if the Blacks were to surrender, their chances of living would be slim. Besides Benson, there were only three other Black policemen around the farmyard. They would have their work cut out for them if they tried to stop the white officers from taking out their revenge on the few living Blacks.

As Benson watched, the tank opened fire. Where a neat white cabin had been, there was now only ruins. The people inside didn't stand a chance. Before the other Black people in the other cabins could realize what was happening the other tank opened fire. It was now a complete massacre. To the white army men inside the tanks, it was a game, something like maneuvers. They had no thought about the Black men and women they were killing.

Suddenly, from one of the few remaining cabins, two Black women and one man came out the front door with their hands over their heads. Before they had taken four steps, they were cut down by a hail of bullets from policemen stationed safely behind the police cars. The people who tried to give themselves up were shot down like mad dogs.

From the barn, Dickie and Shortman and Victor had witnessed everything. "I guess you guys got the message now," Dickie said loudly as his voice shook. "These honkies are playing for keeps. Ain't no surrender, no kind of way. If we don't fight our way out we ain't going to get out." He twisted his neck around and yelled into the barn. "Ain't you bitches got them horses saddled yet?"

"Give us just a few more seconds," Peggy answered.

Dickie turned back toward the scene in the farmyard. "We ain't goin' have no more seconds," he screamed; this time panic was in his voice. "Them fuckin' tanks are beginning to come this way!"

Shortman jumped up from the ground as Victor laid down some covering fire. As soon as Shortman reached the barn entrance, Victor followed.

"We got to get the fuck out of here right now," Vic stated as he ran inside the barn.

As soon as the two women brought horses out, someone would take one. Peggy pulled the horses over to Dickie. "These are the ones I saddled for us," she said, as she noticed the fright in her man's face.

"Quick," Dickie yelled, "somebody get that back door open. We goin' to make our break that way!"

Vic and Shortman wasted no time. The other woman, Irene, leaped up on the horse she was saddling. Another girl, Donna, pushed the heavy rear barn door open, then ran to the horse she had tied near the door.

All six of the Black men and women made their

way out the rear door, each riding a good horse. Before they had cleared the back corral, a shell from one of the tanks burst the barn wide open. The place went up in smoke and fire. The sound of the heavy explosion caused the horses to spook. The one Irene was riding began to buck, but her fear was so great that she stuck to the horse like a burr.

Dickie led the way to the rear of the corral and opened the gate that led away from the farmyard. Their luck was holding because no policemen had spotted them yet. Before all of them had cleared the gate, five policemen came running around the building and saw them trying to make their escape. A yell of alarm went up, and soon other policemen came rushing to the rear. Two police cars roared around the building, but the ground was too chopped up for the cars to follow the horses.

Before they could clear the range of the tanks, one of the tanks came around the building and took aim. The shell exploded about twenty feet away from the fleeing horsemen. The shock of the shell bursting knocked Shortman right out of the saddle. The other five horsemen kept on going.

Dickie rode the horse he was on like he had never ridden before. His heart was beating so fast he thought it would burst. In his mind he knew this was the most frightened he had ever been in his life. In front of them were a line of trees. If he could only reach them they would have a good chance of getting away. Kenyatta had laid out an escape route for them long ago, and Dickie was thankful now that he had paid attention to it.

He glanced back once at his woman, who was riding just as hard as he was. She yelled something to him, but because of the pace of the horses, he couldn't understand what she was trying to say. He turned around in his saddle and concentrated on some hard riding. "Just a few more feet, Lord," he prayed, not aware that he was really talking out loud.

At the sight of Shortman getting knocked clean off his saddle, Victor bent down lower and rode harder. No matter how hard he rode, he couldn't seem to gain on Dickie and Peggy.

One of the police cars with five policemen in it came crashing through the cornfields, trying to cut the horsemen off. When the officers saw that they wouldn't be able to reach the riders, the driver pulled up quickly. One of the officers in the rear yelled, "We got them in rifle range! Let's try pickin' them off." As soon as the car came to a bumping stop, two of the policemen with rifles jumped out and ran around to the hood of the car. They rested their rifles on the hot steel and took dead aim.

The first shot they fired was a miss, but the second officer was a sharpshooter. He never let his aim leave the rider he had picked out.

As Donna bent over and struck her horse on the side, trying to get more speed out of it, she felt something go past her face. She started to glance back, but suddenly something struck her in the middle of her back and lifted her from the saddle. Before she struck the ground, she was dead.

When the policemen saw the rider fall, they let out a yell and began to dance around the car as if they were at a party.

Victor rode past her, knowing as he passed that there was nothing he could do for the woman. A ball of hatred rose up in his throat as he saw the woman he loved lying out on the ground. Even as he rode, he prayed for the strength, to one day be able to make the pigs pay for what they had done this day.

When they reached the woods, Dickie led the way through them. They had to slow the horses down to a walk, but it was okay. For now they weren't on their trail. They had a few minutes, and Dickie believed that was all they needed. If everything was like Kenyatta had left it, they had a good chance of getting away. The four people rode in silence. Nobody bothered to ask Dickie where he was going. They just followed.

After about ten minutes, Dickie came out at a rundown cabin with a dilapidated barn behind it. He dismounted from his horse and directed the rest of the group to do the same thing. He led the way to the barn and opened the sagging doors. Inside was an old station wagon. Dickie got in and opened the ashtray. Sure enough, inside the ashtray were the keys to the car. He let out a sigh of relief as the rest of his small group climbed in. For a second, the station wagon didn't want to start, but finally the motor caught and everybody began to breathe easier.

Dickie lit a cigarette before putting the car in gear. "I'd say it's too hot for us back in Detroit, so from here we're going on to Chicago and from there we'll wait at the hideout until Kenyatta reached us."

Nobody bothered to answer. Each person in the car was too thankful to be alive, let alone have something to complain about. It didn't matter where they went, just as long as they got the hell away from there.

Back at the farmyard, Detective Benson glanced around at the slaughter. The superintendent was now taking charge, since all the fireworks were over. As he watched, Benson wondered about the sharp feeling of pride that went through him as he saw all the dead bodies of his comrades. As he watched, the survivors lined the eight slain officers up side by side. Ambulances rolled in and out of the yard, carrying away the wounded to the nearby hospitals. At least, those brothers made them pay a dear price for their victory. With eight policemen killed, the newspapers would play it up big. This was the first time to his memory that any Black or white crooks had ever made such a dent in the police forces at a single shoot-out. Instantly he felt ashamed of the feeling of pride in what the Black men and women had done. After all, he was an officer also, and these were his comrades, so there was nothing to be proud about. Eight of his fellow officers lay dead, and there had been a good chance of him being one of those with a sheet over his head.

If he needed anything to justify his feelings, the sight of the tanks being reloaded on the trucks gave it to him. The use of the tanks had left a very bitter taste in his mouth, but it had been the right thing to do. Why waste lives when you could call up such help? If the tanks had been there at first, none of the men lying under the blankets would be dead now.

"Those fuckin' tanks were lifesavers, weren't they?" Ryan said as he came up beside his partner. Benson, taken by surprise, glanced around at his partner quickly, hoping Ryan couldn't read what he was sure was showing in his face.

"Yeah," Benson answered, "if it hadn't have been for those tanks, it might have cost us more men than it did."

"You can say that again," Ryan replied. "Those bastards didn't know the meaning of quit."

His words brought a sharp fleeting pain to Benson, because he remembered all too well what happened to the ones who tried to quit. They had been shot down like mad dogs. He wondered what the outcome would have been had the people in the cabins been all white. Would they have used tanks and flame throwers on them then? Benson shook his head, trying to shake off the useless thoughts.

Ryan stared at his partner in surprise, wondering what was disturbing him. "I know this was a messy thing out here, Ben, but if you want, we can get the hell away. A few of those people made it to the woods, but we don't have to worry about it. The sheriff and his men are throwing up roadblocks all around the woods, so once they leave the damn horses, they'll be caught like fish in a fuckin' barrel."

"Yeah, I know," Benson answered more sharply than he intended. "Since they'll be the only Black things out here on foot, it shouldn't be too hard to spot them out on the highway trying to get a fuckin' lift!"

"Hey man," Ryan said quietly, "take it easy. I know this wasn't easy on you, but these fuckin' guys got what they deserved. They're responsible for I don't know how many policemen's lives, so if you want to feel sorry for somebody, how about feeling sorry for some of the police widows these bastards caused!"

Benson forced himself to grin. "I got you, man. Just overlook me for a few minutes, okay? Those tanks were kind of hard to take. I saw what kind of damage they did, and it's just hard to accept, that's all."

For a minute both officers were silent. The sun was just beginning to go down and the activity in the farmyard was an eyeful by itself.

Television men now ran back and forth, while their camera crews followed, lugging their heavy equipment. Before any of the television newsmen could reach them, Ryan pulled his partner's arm.

"Let's get in our car and head downtown. The captain says he wants to see us right away. I think they have a very special mission for us coming up."

"Special huh," Benson replied and snorted. "I'll just bet it's special. What the fuck do they want us to do, go down to the morgue and identify the remains of half of these bodies that's been burned damn near to a crisp?"

Again Detective Ryan gave his partner that funny look out of the corner of his eye. Something was disturbing the hell out of Benson, that he was sure of, but he just couldn't put his finger on what it was.

4

———

KENYATTA STEPPED OUT of the cockpit. The first thing he saw was an abundance of dead bodies. He stared at one corpse especially. It was his friend Zeke. He and Zeke had done a lot of things together, and it hurt deeply to see his life-long friend stretched out cold on the floor of the airplane. As people came running up to him with silly questions, Kenyatta waved them away. He continued on through the plane, stopping to examine the wound that Red had in his shoulder. He leaned over and tore Red's shirt so that he could get a better look at the ugly wound.

"Is there a doctor anywhere on the plane?" he asked sharply, his eyes searching the passengers' faces.

A short, red-faced white man got up from his

seat and came forward. "Yes, I'm a doctor," the man stated.

"Good, then do what you can for my friend here," Kenyatta ordered, then continued on his way through the airplane. When he reached the rear of the plane, Betty stared into the eyes of her man. They looked at each other closely, then Kenyatta spoke. "Sugar, find out if any of these fuckin' stewardesses know how to let down the emergency ladder from this plane. We going to have to start walking. Then," he continued, "after that, find out how much water is on this fuckin' plane and see to it that some of our people take control of it. We goin' need every drop of it more than likely, 'cause we're on the motherfucker fuckin' desert."

"Damn," Betty cursed, then quickly walked toward the nearest stewardess to follow out her man's order.

Kenyatta made his way back up the aisle. He stopped and glanced down at Ann. He knew at once that she was dead. He cursed under his breath, as he wondered how the hell things got so far out of control while he was in the cockpit. There was no sense in him trying to fault someone. It was over and done. Nothing he could say would bring the dead back to life. Whoever was responsible would carry the blame on his mind from now on. Somebody had been careless. It was the only explanation for things getting out of control the way they did. When he had gone into the cockpit, everything had been in order.

Kenyatta then noticed the two dead white men and the guns they held. Suddenly he knew what had happened. The whiteys had taken his group by surprise. The way he saw it, it couldn't have happened any other way.

Eddie-Bee came running up to Kenyatta. "Man, we are in one hell of a fix, Kenyatta. What the fuck are we goin' do about it?"

Kenyatta glanced at the smaller man, wishing that he had been killed instead of his reliable friend Zeke. "Don't get upset," Kenyatta said, not letting his thoughts show. "If you want something to do, go to the rear of the plane and give Betty a hand." Before Eddie-Bee could ask any more questions Kenyatta quickly walked past the man. He noticed the dead Black woman and again wondered just how the hell she had died. It must have been a stray bullet, he reasoned, and went on past the grieving threesome.

Jug stood near the cockpit, waiting on Kenyatta. He didn't bother to ask any foolish questions, he just waited silently for his leader to tell him what to do next.

Kenyatta put his arm around Jug's shoulder. "Boy," he began, "we got big problems on our hands, Jug."

Again Jug remained silent, waiting for Kenyatta to continue. "We goin' have to leave this fuckin' plane out here in the middle of nowhere, man. I'm havin' the women collect all the water we can carry, so maybe we won't have any water problem, but the damn problem is I don't know where the fuck we are. Except for being on the desert, I don't have the goddamnest idea of where we are at this moment!"

Jug smiled slightly. "If anybody can pull us out of this shit, Ken," he stated, "you can. So just keep the faith, boy, just keep the faith."

Kenyatta smiled at Jug, then spoke up loudly so the rest of the men and women in his group could hear. "We are gettin' ready to leave this airplane, so take whatever you think you might need. Any of you girls that were wearing high heel shoes that are hard to walk in, exchange them with some of the passengers. No telling how damn far we might have to walk. Flat bottom shoes will be ideal for what's in front of us."

"Ken, honey," Betty called to him from the rear of the airplane, "we have the ladder down now. It's not as easy as the ramp was to come up, but all of us should be able to go down it without too much damn trouble." She spoke in a matter-of-fact voice.

"Okay then, I guess we had better start making some kind of preparations to get Red down the ladder," Kenyatta said as he walked over to where the doctor was still working on Red's shoulder.

"Hey, man," he said as he bent down over Red, "how the hell do you feel?"

Red glanced up at him and tried to smile. "Shit, Kenyatta, I been hurt worse than this by a bite my woman put on me."

The doctor shook his head. "This man is in no shape to be trying to make a trip across any desert," he stated with authority.

"Well, doc," Kenyatta replied, "he might not be in any shape, but I'll bet he'll be better off with us than waiting for the law to come and pick him up and take him to the nearest fuckin' prison hospital. No, we ain't about to leave him here for some shit like that. You people will be rescued more than likely before dusk tomorrow, but the only thing Red would have waiting for him would be a prison cell. Doc, if you got any heavy drugs in that bag of yours, please leave them with us. Maybe if we can keep him drugged enough, he won't feel the pain so bad. It's goin' be hell out there for all of us, but it's our only chance, and we ain't about to pass it up."

Kenyatta glanced up and down the plane. "Betty, see if you can find some kind of stretcher or something so we can carry Red."

"Will do," she called back, her voice sounding cheerful under the circumstances.

Jug walked over to the automatic ladder that had been let down. "You want I should go down and take a quick look around, Ken?" he inquired.

"Good idea, baby boy, damn good idea," Kenyatta yelled back. "Check out everything you can see, then come on back up and give me the fuckin' lowdown on it."

Kenyatta watched the tall, dark-complexioned man disappear out the opened side door. It seemed like little more than seconds had passed before Jug was jumping back through the door, his face lit up with excitement. "Hey, Kenyatta," he yelled out. "We goin' have company in a minute. I seen and heard some goddamn motorcycles coming this way. It looked to be at least five of them!"

"Hummm," Kenyatta snorted, then added, "cool on that. Yes sirree, cool on that. Looks like we might not have to walk off this fuckin' desert after all." He glanced at his followers and all of their faces were turned toward him expectantly.

"What we'll do," he began, "is wait until they get here, then we'll fake like we're passengers until we can get the drop on them. After that, we'll just let them join the passengers up here while we use their bikes to get the fuck out of here. I hope enough of you know how to ride a fuckin' bike, because if you don't, you're going to get some damn quick lessons on it." He smiled, taking the sting out of his words.

"I still say," the doctor said as he came up to Kenyatta, "that this boy on the floor is hurt too bad to attempt to try and take him out of here. If you do, his death will be on your conscience."

Kenyatta grinned at the man. "If I don't, his confinement will be on my goddamn mind from now on, doc, so I ain't got much choice. In fact I'll leave the choice up to Red. He's awake, ask him what the hell does he want to do. Stay here and await medical attention, or take his chances with us?"

The doctor glanced down at the stricken man. Red grinned up at him. "He's running it to you right, doc. I thank you for what you've done, man, but ain't no way no sore shoulder is goin' keep me here until Johnnie Law arrives. No sir, I'll take my chances out there on the desert with the rest of my people. Shit, once my people leave, what the hell do I know what will happen. These mad-ass passengers just might try taking their anger out on me, and then I'd be in one hell of a fix, wouldn't I?"

For an answer, the doctor shrugged his shoulders and returned to his seat. He didn't bother to leave any drugs.

"Hey, doc," Kenyatta yelled, "didn't you forget something?"

Before the doctor could answer, Kenyatta continued. "I asked you to leave us some drugs, something that would kill the pain for my man here. Now if you want to act shitty, we can take you along with us to take care of him!"

The threat was enough. The doctor opened his bag quickly and removed some pink and white pills. "These are very strong pain pills. In fact," the doctor continued, "they are habit forming if a person takes them too often."

"Let us do the worrying about the habit forming bit, doc. You just set that shit out," Kenyatta ordered. Betty called from her spot near the ladder. "Honey, the bikes are damn near here."

It was unnecessary for her to say anything because everybody on the airplane could hear the motorcycles as they came roaring up. Kenyatta rushed to the ladder and began to climb down. And as he climbed he could see six bikes swinging around near the side of the huge 707 airplane.

"Hey, what it is!" Kenyatta called out in his most cheerful voice as he came down the ladder. "Are we glad to see you people, we thought we were down over no-man's-land!"

A tall, blond-headed man with hair down to his shoulders spoke up. "You damn near are. What happened, did the plane crash?"

"Naw, man," Kenyatta stated as he dropped smoothly to the ground. "The pilot had engine trouble so he had to set her down the best place he could. By the way," Kenyatta continued, "where the hell are we?"

One of the other bikers spoke up. "You're about a hundred miles from Las Vegas and three hundred from Los Angeles, buddy."

"It's that bad, huh?" Kenyatta asked, studying

the group of people in front of him. He noticed at once that two of the bike riders were women.

"Well, what the hell are you people doing so far away from everything?" Kenyatta asked, wondering where their camp could be.

"Oh, it's not as bad as it seems," one of the women said, as she tossed her long red hair back out of her face. "There's a ranch just over those sand hills. We saw your plane coming in, so we started riding out this way."

The blond-headed man cut his eyes at her sharply, before he spoke up. "What's wrong with the rest of the passengers? Can't any of them climb down the ladder?"

"Oh," Kenyatta said, then laughed, "yeah, man, it's a few men up there who can climb down, but the women don't want to come down until I've found out what's going on."

"Just who the hell are you?" the blond man asked sharply. From the tone of his voice, Kenyatta could tell that he was one of those that couldn't stand a Black man.

"I happen to be the guard on this plane," Kenyatta answered sharply. "The pilot was hurt during the landing so it's my job to find out just what the hell is going on before I can allow the passengers to come down. We are paid to protect the passengers at all costs. I guess you understand where I'm coming from."

A few of the people on their bikes nodded their

heads. Then Kenyatta added the clincher. "If any of you want to go up now, it's okay with me. I just don't feel up to the climb right this minute, you dig?"

Before anyone could take him up on his offer, Jug came climbing down the ladder. The white people on the motorcycles stared coldly at the second Black man.

Kenyatta bowed and held out his hand. "Be my guest, and go on up and look for yourselves. The lady stewardess will fill you in on anything I've left out. Now," he said, turning directly toward the red-headed woman, "I'd like to know a little more about this ranch you spoke of. Do you think it could handle as many people as we have aboard this plane, and would it be a very difficult walk for some of them? You know, all of the passengers aren't as young as we are," he stated and then winked at her.

Her sharp laugh rang out and seemed to irritate the tall blond man. He cursed, then climbed off his bike. "I think I'll just climb up the ladder and see what the hell is going on," he stated, and stared coldly at Kenyatta, as if he wanted him to try and prevent him from going up the ladder.

"Help yourself," Kenyatta said. "Maybe, you can even help some of the older people down while you're up there."

The blond man didn't bother to answer. He

just began to climb the ladder swiftly. In seconds he was making his way through the open hatchway. Before any of the other bike riders could get set, Kenyatta and Jug set themselves so that they surrounded the bikes.

As soon as the tall white man entered the airplane he knew something was wrong. The first sight that greeted him was that of dead bodies lying around in the aisles. He cursed as he stared at the sight. "What the shit!"

"Just take it easy, daddy," Betty said as she slipped up beside him. "You just take it easy and call one of your other friends up here."

"The hell you say," the man swore and then made a quick grab at the gun in her hand.

Betty took one step back and pulled the trigger. The hard-hitting magnum knocked the tall blond man off his feet. Before he hit the ground she had pumped another round into his body.

"Shit," Betty swore, "it could have went so easy if the bastard had only had some sense!"

The sound of the gunshot was somewhat muffled but not enough so that the people on the ground didn't hear it. They stood looking up at the plane.

"What the hell's going on up there?" one of the male bike riders inquired.

Kenyatta removed his gun and held it on the people. "I'll tell you what," Kenyatta stated, "you start climbing up the ladder, then you can call back down and let your friends know just what's happening up there."

The man Kenyatta had spoken to stared at the gun in the Black man's hand, then at the ladder. "Hey, buddy," he began, "I don't give a shit what's going on up there. I'll just start my bike up and get the fuck out of here and leave this party to you people."

The bullet from Jug's gun took the man in the side of the head. He never knew what hit him. Jug stared around at the rest of the bike riders. His eyes were cold.

"Well now," Kenyatta said, "looks like he won't do any more bike riding for a hell of a long time. You," Kenyatta ordered, pointing his gun at one of the other men, "get to climbing."

The man didn't waste any time. He jumped off his bike and raced for the ladder. He went up like a monkey, never bothering to look back as fear added speed to his arms and legs. When he entered the airplane Betty was waiting for him. He took one glance at his friend stretched out on the floor of the airplane and stuck his hands in the air.

"Please don't shoot," he begged. "Your friend down on the ground told me to come up. Other than that, I don't want to know nothing about what's going on here."

Betty smiled at the man. "Well now," she said, "you seem to have the right idea on how to survive. You just keep thinking that away. Now you find you a seat somewheres and I'm sure won't nothing happen to you."

Before the words were out of her mouth, the man hurried over to an empty seat and balled up in it. He dropped his head down on his chest as though he were asleep, but everybody could see his shoulders shaking from fear.

Back on the ground, Kenyatta turned to the only remaining man. "Now then, friend, I'd like to have a little more information on this ranch you say that's just over the hill. How many people are still there?"

As soon as the man hesitated, Kenyatta raised his pistol and shot him out of the seat of the bike. "I guess we can do without a slow thinker. Anybody who has to take that long to think shouldn't be living."

The two women shivered as they watched the cold-blooded killing. "Now then," Kenyatta said, turning to the redheaded woman. "I'm going to ask you some easy questions, and it's up to you whether or not you live. If I think you're lying, I'm going to blow your shit out, is that clear?"

The redheaded woman could only shake her head in agreement. "I'll do my best," she replied, her voice shaking.

"Now, baby," Kenyatta answered her. "You're going to do better than your best. You're going to tell me the fuckin' truth or die, is that clear?"

It was all too clear. She again shook her head. "Yes, I understand," she mumbled.

"Okay, then, now we understand each other," Kenyatta said easily, as he took out his smokes and lit one. "First of all, I want to know how many people are still at the ranch."

"There's five people left there," she answered quickly.

"What are they, men or women?" Kenyatta asked.

"There's three women and two men left at the ranch," she answered him instantly.

Kenyatta smiled. "Good, that's just fine, honey. You don't have to worry. If you just keep on being for real, you'll come out of this shit all right. In fact, I promise you, you'll come up smelling like a rose."

The other woman, a slim, black-haired girl, held onto the handlebars of her bike as though her life depended on it. She glanced from one Black man to the other.

Jug walked over to the black-haired girl and nudged her in the ribs with his gun. "Is she telling the truth?" he asked sharply, as he leaned over and stared in her face.

The woman was so scared she could only move her head up and down. As Jug stood there, he noticed a puddle of water beginning to run off the bike and knew that the woman had actually pissed on herself in fright.

"I think they're tellin' the real, Ken," Jug said

as he walked back away from the woman, grinning.

"I think so, too," Kenyatta replied. "It sounds so damn good, it's hard to believe. Here we land in the fuckin' middle of nowhere, and now we got a goddamn dude ranch right next door to us, waiting for us to take it over. Hey Red," Kenyatta called out, "who's the fuckin' owner of this joint, huh?"

First the redheaded woman pointed upward with her head, then managed to say, "The blond man who went up into the airplane first."

"Oh," Kenyatta drew the word out, "shit, then we ain't got no problems, 'cause his next of kin will have to worry 'bout the ranch. He's past the worrying stage."

Suddenly Betty came climbing down the ladder; she moved with the sureness of a man. When she reached the bottom she took in the two women and her eyes became slits. "What's happenin' down here, daddy?" she inquired as she tossed a look at the redhead that promised trouble down the road.

"Nothing, honey, we're just gettin a little information, that's all." Kenyatta replied, ignoring the obvious jealousy of his mate.

"Well," Betty stated coldly as she posed with her hands on her hips, "if you're havin' trouble out of the bitches, why don't you let me handle it? I'm sure they will be glad to talk to me."

Kenyatta laughed loudly. "It's just the opposite, baby, we ain't havin' no kinds of problems whatsoever. The ladies are being very helpful."

Betty glared first at one woman, then at the next one. It was written in her eyes what she wanted to do. The magnum in her hand twitched as she nervously handled it. She finally glanced back up at Kenyatta. "Well, just what the hell are we supposed to do, just sit out here forever?"

Kenyatta stared at her coldly. "Now don't get beside yourself for nothing, baby. I'll take care of everything. When I get all the information I want, then we will make a move. Until then, just play it cool."

"I guess you want me to go back up on the airplane while you finish gettin' your information, right, Kenyatta?" Betty asked sharply.

"Wrong, bitch, I don't give a shit if you dig a motherfuckin' hole in this sand and crawl in it. But whatever you do," Kenyatta stated, "you better get your mind right, 'cause this ain't no fuckin' game! Now if you want to stay, don't act shitty, because there's no reason for it. These girls are really being helpful, and I don't want you fuckin' them over for nothing!"

His words brought a small bit of relief to both the white women, because it was obvious that the tall Black woman wouldn't like anything better than to cut them down with the pistol she carried.

"Jug," Kenyatta spoke quietly, "you go back up

in the plane and have our people collect every weapon up there. Then have them start coming down one at a time. We're going to move to the ranch. But before you do anything, be sure the fuckin' radio on the airplane is ripped out so that nobody can put it together again. You got that?" Kenyatta inquired as the tall Black man started to leave. Jug stopped and nodded his head, then continued on his way.

After the departure of Jug, Betty relaxed a little. She listened quietly as Kenyatta inquired about the ranch and the nearest town. As far as they could find out, there wasn't a soul within fifty miles. It was ideal. They would have plenty of time to make their escape before anybody had the slightest idea where they were.

"You say there's three cars at the ranch," Kenyatta asked again. The redheaded woman nodded her head. "Yes, plus four dune buggies that we use on the desert."

"Wonderful," Kenyatta stated as he clapped his hands in glee. "Betty, baby, it couldn't have been any sweeter! Girl, we got Jesus in a jug, woman, and you can't even see it!"

"I see it, but how the fuck do we know what the truth is? This bitch could be lying, you know," Betty stated coldly.

At the sound of her words, Kenyatta just shook his head. "Goddamn it, woman, if she's lying, she knows damn well I'm going to kill her, so you can bet your ass she ain't hardly doing that. Red wants to live too bad, don't you, Red?"

The tall redheaded woman could only nod her head. The sight of the tall Black woman gave her more fear than she had felt when both Black men had been talking to her. She believed she could handle them, but the woman was another matter. For the slightest reason the woman would kill her, and the redhead knew it. Fear gripped her entire body. She could not stop her legs from shaking.

It didn't take long before the rest of the small group began to come down the ladder. Jug had carried out his orders to a tee. He was the last one down the ladder, waiting patiently until the two people helping the wounded Red brought him down the ladder. The doctor had given him a shot of morphine—keeping the wounded man from feeling too much pain as he was carried down the ladder.

When they reached the ground they gathered around Kenyatta, each one with a different question.

"What about the passengers?" one of his group asked from the background.

"Don't worry about them," Kenyatta replied. "We sent one man up there from the ranch, so he can lead them over there sometime tomorrow. It ain't far, just a few hours walk. They will make out all right."

"As for us," Kenyatta continued, "we're going to take over the ranch for a minute, then given the right break, we'll strike out for the promised land. Right now, I want everybody who can ride a bike to get on one. Those who can't, get on the rear. We're going to take these two white ladies along with us, so show them the proper respect, hear?"

There was laughter at his warning. The small group got aboard the motorcycles and began the trip across the sand dunes.

5

AS EVENING APPROACHED, Dickie and his small group were making their fantastic getaway. Dickie and Victor were the only two men remaining, while Peggy and Irene were the only women to escape the massacre. Out of over forty people these were the only ones left. It had been almost a total wipeout.

The occupants of the car discussed the shootout as they drove away. It was on everybody's mind. Irene, sitting in the backseat next to Victor, stared out of the window, fear riding her every thought.

"You think we goin' make it?" she asked, her voice shaking with fear.

"Don't even worry about it," Dickie replied. "The pigs are looking for some niggers in the woods riding horses. They ain't even set up roadblocks yet. By the time they get around to it," he continued, "we goin' be so far away they won't know us from any other Black people."

"That's right," Peggy said. "They don't know what we look like, so we ain't got no problem. Once we get clear of this area, we shouldn't have anything to worry about."

"Hey," Victor yelled from the backseat, "she has got a point there. If we didn't have these guns in the car and they stopped us, we could play from under it. Ain't no way they can put us at that farmhouse."

Dickie drove on in silence, thinking about what Victor had just said. As he neared the highway, he pulled over. "Vic, take them rifles and pistols and put them over there in the bushes. Be sure to wipe off whatever prints might be on them. We goin' play it like you said. So if we get stopped, we're just a square couple out havin' a fuckin' ride for the day, dig it?"

"Yeah baby, if everybody remembers it that away we ain't got no problems. No problems at all," Vic said.

The tension in the car was high. Everybody could feel their nerves jumping. It had been more than close. Each and every one of them were lucky to still be alive, and they all knew it.

"Goddamn," Peggy said. "Did you dig them motherfuckin' tanks? I ain't never seen anything like it before. Them motherfuckin' pigs killed Pete and the rest of them like dogs. They didn't stand a chance!"

The four people in the car fell silent while Victor took his time and wiped the guns clean of any prints that might have been on the guns they had used. When he got out of the car, Dickie watched in the car mirror until Victor returned from hiding the guns.

"I placed them well back in the weeds, man," Victor stated as he climbed back in the car. He was breathing hard, as though he had just finished a long-distance race. "With a little luck, won't nobody find them for a few days or weeks."

"That will be just fine for us," Dickie said, "but regardless of what happens now, I don't know a fuckin' thing about them. I ain't seen no rifles, if you know what I mean."

Everybody in the car laughed. It was a little relief from the pressure they had all been under. Now they could relax and breathe easier. Even if they were stopped, there was no evidence against them. It was doubtful if any police could really identify any of them as the Blacks who had been at the farm.

As far as Dickie was concerned, he knew now that he had a good chance of getting away. Since he had never been arrested with any of the other members he stood a good chance of not being discovered. Even as he thought about it, he had to shake off the jitters. Whoever was caught had big troubles on their hands, because the pigs would toss the book at them. Murder in the first degree would be the charge, he had no doubt about that. Too many police had been killed. He had seen four cops go down that he knew of.

"Yeah, momma, you said a mouthful," Vic said. "Them fuckin' tanks sent shivers down my goddamn spine! Did you see what that fuckin' flamethrower did to the cabin Jim and Lacy were in?"

It went like that as Dickie drove onto the highway. They rehashed the events of the afternoon. It was as though they couldn't talk about anything else. It was the only thing on any of their minds.

Irene began to cry softly. "Why don't you turn on the radio or something, Dickie? I've had enough reminders of what happened. I wish ya would find something else to talk about. What happened was too gruesome for us to keep kickin' it around," she stated as tears began to roll down her lovely brown cheeks. Irene was a medium-sized woman, well shaped with a teasingly tanned complexion. She could pass for a schoolteacher any day of the week if she so wished. Whenever she smiled, she revealed well kept teeth that were as white as freshly fallen snow, while her hair was an auburn brown that came out of the neighborhood drugstore.

At her suggestion Dickie turned on the radio. As soon as a popular hit blues number went off, the news came on. Everybody in the car became quiet as the commentator began to talk about the hijacking of an airplane by a group of militant Blacks. The newsman continued, giving descriptions of the Black men and woman who had commandeered the plane.

"Sonofabitch!" Victor cursed. The slim Black man looked as though he was about to have a stroke as he continued to listen. "Sonofabitch," he said over and over again. "It just couldn't be." The very thought was almost too much for him.

"It couldn't be anybody else but them," Dickie said firmly. "Just who in the hell else could it be? Shit, from the descriptions it has to be Kenyatta. It couldn't be that many tall, Black, baldheaded men in the city with enough nerve to take over a fuckin' airplane!"

"If it is them," Peggy began, "it seems as if they could have wired us up on it. Shit, Dickie, from where I sit, it looks as if we were played for goddamn fools. While we hold the pigs off, they make their news-shattering escape. Shit," she continued, "it looks as if we were used for fools and tools, tying the pigs up with an old-fashioned shoot-out while the king and his personal handpicked friends made their getaway."

"Aw, baby," Dickie said quietly as his mind raced wildly, "why don't you think positive instead of coming up with that abstract shit? If it was the big man, Kenyatta, it still don't mean he used us. I'll bet he didn't know anything about the pigs getting ready to hit the farm. If he had, honey, don't think for a minute he wouldn't have taken the time to pull our coats about it."

"Yeah, girl," Vic said, adding his little bit. "Don't even imagine that Kenyatta would have left all of us up tight. If he had only known about it, he would have pulled our coats so that we could have been ready for them pigs. It's our own fault, we should have been ready." Victor pulled out his cigarettes and crumpled up the pack after cursing when he found it empty.

"After all the training we been put through," Victor continued, "we should have been more damn prepared than what we were. As it was, we went into action too late. The first pigs that showed up should have been wiped completely out. If we had took care like we been trained to, the first two or three carloads shouldn't even of had the time to call their fuckin' partners!"

"Quiet!" Irene ordered loudly as the speaker on the radio came back with some more news. The announcer's voice filled the car as Dickie raised the volume on the car radio.

"From our latest reports," the commentator went on, "it's believed that the hijackers of the Boeing 707 were members of a highly organized gang of militant Blacks who had a deadly shoot-out at a farmhouse located in the backwoods of Middleton township. After the smoke had cleared, there were seven policemen dead, while nine others were rushed to the nearest hospital because of wounds received in the shootout. An accurate count of the Black people killed was impossible because of the use of highly powerful flame-throwers, which left no remains."

As the foursome in the car listened, the news-cast continued. "While there was no accurate count, there were over twenty-five Blacks believed to be killed."

"Goddamn, goddamn, goddamn," Victor mur-mured over and over again. The slim, brown skinned man was deeply hurt by the incident. There were tears of frustration rolling down his cheeks as he fell silent.

"At the latest report," the announcer continued in a louder voice, seemingly becoming enraged by the news he was reading, "even after such a large death count of the militant Blacks, the police are searching the immediate area for a least four or five other Blacks that got away during the violent shoot-out. The police are warning everybody not to approach these people as they are highly dan-gerous. Some farmers in the area have armed themselves in hopes of collecting a reward off the arrest of these mad dogs. But the warning from the police is that these people are highly danger-ous, and to avoid them at all costs. If you should by chance see some Blacks hitchhiking on the highway, do not, and I restate, do not pick them up. Your life will be worthless if you should be-cause they think nothing of killing, and now that they are on the run, they are even more dangerous!"

There was a brief interruption while the announcer spoke of some product, but in seconds he was back speaking of the shoot-out. "There is no reward, I repeat, there is no reward on these people, so don't try and be heroes. If by chance you see them, notify your nearest policeman." He hesitated a moment, then added. "Now don't forget, over seven police have died because of these people, so I can't even find the words to express to you how dangerous these mad dogs are."

"Mad dogs my ass," Dickie swore. "He ain't said nothing about the use of the fuckin' tanks, of killin' Black men and women like fuckin' dogs! Naw, the whitey ain't goin' come out with the real. I just wish I could get him in front of my gunsight, then I'd sure enough let him know just how fuckin' mad we are!"

There was a general agreement from the other people in the car. All of them would have loved a crack at the big mouth announcer.

"I wonder about that shit that happened on the airplane. If it was Kenyatta or not," Peggy stated, as she rubbed her chin. "It just don't seem possible, but the way they described the people it sure as hell sounded like our man."

"You can say that again," Victor said. Suddenly everybody froze as a police car went speeding past. The officers inside the car didn't even bother to glance in their direction. "Goddamn," Victor continued, "this kind of shit will give me a damn heart attack!"

"It won't be long now," Dickie said, as he made

a right turn. The freeway was right ahead. Everybody in the car relaxed more.

After taking another look in his mirror, Dickie turned onto the ramp that led down onto the freeway. "It won't be long now," he said. "When we pull up, well be in Chicago. These motherfuckers won't have the damnedest idea of which way we went."

"Another bulletin came in just now," the white announcer stated. "Captain Dillard, one of the more important officers on the case, has called in and reassured us that the apprehension of the wildly fleeing Blacks will come soon. He doesn't give them a chance of escaping the area, which has been sealed off. Every car with Black men and women in it is under surveillance. Captain Dillard states that a field mouse couldn't get through the net they have thrown up with over five hundred men."

"Hey man, wow!" Irene screamed. "They really ain't holding back, are they?"

Dickie laughed. "Shit, five hundred and five hundred motherfuckin' more ain't even enough! We have went through their goddamn roadblocks now. Even if they stopped us, we're just innocent Blacks on our way to Chi, to visit friends. Shit, they don't have the slightest idea of what we look like. I pity any Blacks out that away who just happen to be joy riding. Their ass is going to get jacked up!"

"You can say that again," Victor added, as he

stared out the window moodily. "I'm going to make a pig pay for this shit one day, you can bet on it!"

"That's two of us," Dickie answered, as he moved the car smoothly in and out of the evening traffic.

Back at the farmhouse Detective Ryan and his Black partner Benson prepared to leave. Benson had had enough of the funny stares his fellow officers were tossing his way. They seemed to think that because he was Black, he was sort of responsible for what had happened. He gritted his teeth until his jaw muscles stood out. He glared back at a tall red-faced detective who kept looking at him.

Benson shook his head, then stated, "You had better start this fuckin' wagon up. Ryan, before we end up havin' another fuckin' dead officer on our hands!"

Without replying Ryan started the car. He had noticed the frustration in his partner's face and he knew the cause. He wished that he knew how to pacify his friend, but it was out of his hands. The behavior of some stupid asses wasn't his fault. Yet in a way, he did feel responsible.

"Come on, brother," he began, "It's farcical for me to pretend that I didn't see some of them stupid cocksuckers rolling their fuckin' eyes at you, Ben, but fuck man, this ain't the first time so don't let it pull you down."

Benson let out a loud laugh that was completely against his nature. "Yeah, I dig where you're coming from, but it's hard to just ignore that kind of shit when I just finished putting my mother-fuckin' life on the line! Those same bastards who are looking so fuckin' disturbed are the same ones who were five hundred feet in the rear, safely behind somebody's goddamn car."

"What the shit," Ryan replied. "Those guys aren't nothing but fuckin' poot butts, because if they weren't, they'd know who the fuck you were on sight."

"Big deal!" Benson said, then crossed his legs and fell silent. The mood he was in was a danger-ous one, yet he didn't want to take his anger out on his white partner. The sight of so many Black bodies had done something to him. At first, he had been sick to his stomach, but after a while he had gotten over that part of it. Death was a part of his life. He came in contact with it more than the average person, so he was damn near immune to it. But for some reason, this time it had gotten to him. Maybe it was the sight of the attractive Black women laid out on the grass. Whatever, he didn't like the taste it had left in his mouth.

Ryan knew his partner well, and when he saw him fall silent, he let the silence hang. Let Ben brood for a while, he'd get over it. He had in the past, so Ryan had no reason to doubt that the man wouldn't this time.

The two men remained silent until they were almost back to the station. Benson didn't speak until Ryan pulled up off the freeway. "Sweet Lord o' mercy, what in the fuck has a Black person got to do to prove to some of these assholes that all Black people aren't like the ones we had the shoot-out with. I personally killed at least two of the Black kids at that farmhouse, but it wasn't enough. No, hell no, just because I'm of the Black race I'm still guilty as hell of what those misguided fools did."

Ryan listened but there was nothing he could say to his partner. Benson would have to get it out of his system his own way. He had seen his partner bitter before but never to the extent that he was now. Benson seemed to be spurred on savagely by something inside him. Whatever it was, it wouldn't give the man any rest.

"Them fuckin' assholes," Benson almost screamed. "How the hell can they hold a whole damn race of people guilty for what a few fuckin' nuts do? If it had been all white people at the farmhouse, it would be different. So goddamn different that I seriously doubt that they would have called in the motherfuckin' army. No tanks, no goddamn way, Ryan. Shit! I don't care how fuckin' hard the damn whites would have fought, do you really think they would have resorted to those fuckin' flamethrowers?"

Benson didn't even wait for a reply. "Hell no!" It was as though he was talking to himself, ignoring the man sitting in the car beside him. He continued in a loud, angry voice. "Never! Not in a million years. They burned those poor misguided niggers up like they were just insects in the fuckin' way."

The tone of voice Benson used revealed the hurt that was so evident inside him. He couldn't hide it if his life depended on it. His words rang in Ryan's ears, causing him to feel self-conscious. He knew in his heart that the Black man had a point, but how could be explain something that was out of his hands? This was one of the reasons why it had been so hard to work with a moody black detective. At times Benson made Ryan ashamed of being white.

"What can I say?" Ryan asked, almost bewildered. "We both know what the deal is, so what the fuck am I supposed to say about it. I'm sorry! Shit! If I said that, it would be a lie, Ben. Those people killed seven policemen. I'm not sorry for their death. Maybe I regret the way they had to be taken out, but I'm damn sure not sorry about it." Ryan hesitated for a minute, then continued. "Hell fire, didn't anyone put guns in their hands and make them take the stand they did. Ben, you got to remember something, while you're lettin' your emotions run away with you. You got to remember that we've been hunting these people for a long time. And all during that time they've been cutting down one white policeman after another. Not to mention other people that they've got some sort of gripe against.

"These people have already set themselves up as some sort of judge and jury, thinking that somebody's given them the right to kill people just because they don't like them. Well I'll tell you something you already know, Ben, and that's that nobody has given them that right. We don't have it and nobody else does. They chose their own life, they also chose the way they wanted it to end. They could have given themselves up. It didn't have to go as far as it did."

The cold, bitter laughter that came from Benson made shivers run up and down Ryan's spine. For a second he wondered if his partner was losing his mind. Then Benson began to speak.

"They could have given themselves up, you say? Where the hell were you when those poor bastards came out of the cabin with their hands in the air. Don't tell me you really missed that part of the show?"

Ryan couldn't look his friend and partner in the eye. He had also witnessed the cold-blooded killing of the few Blacks who had tried to surrender. But again, it was out of his hands. What the hell could he say or do about it?

"Okay, Ben, I saw the gun-happy bastards shoot them down, but now where do we go from here? What do you want from me? Should I file a report about it, and start some paperwork that will get lost some place along the line? But," Ryan continued, "won't the big wheels be happy about it. You know damn well I'll be signing my death warrant, or rather, ending my career as a police officer, because the first time I make a mistake they will hang my ass for bringing up this kind of shit!"

Benson sighed deeply. "Naw, man, I don't want you to put your neck out. What fuckin' good would it do? The people are dead now, so what the fuck. If I filed the goddamned complaint, they would just say I'm a fuckin' silly-ass nigger with a chip on my shoulder. On the other hand, if you filed the complaint, I know they'd fuck around and split us up first, then end up by fucking over you for pulling the covers off their ass. No Ryan, don't pay any attention to me, man, I'm just trying to get it out of my system. It hit me hard tonight for some goddamn reason. I don't know why, and I wish the hell I could quit thinking about it! There's nothing I can do about it, anyway."

By the time Ryan drove into the police garage Benson had managed to get himself under control. He kept telling himself that he would just have to understand them. Understand why some whites just loved killing Blacks. It was just that simple. Once he understood that he might be able to cope with the problem.

The two men took the stairway upstairs to their small office. "Damn," Ryan swore as he sat down behind his tiny desk.

Benson removed his coat, revealing the long shoulder holster where his .38 police special rested snugly. He walked over to the filing cabinet where they kept files on various criminals and informers that they used on different occasions. Without inquiring about it, Benson fixed two cups of coffee and carried the one he had fixed for Ryan over to the desk and set it in front of the man. They sipped their coffee in silence, each man deep in his own private thoughts.

"You know Ben," Ryan began, "this shit ain't about over." He waited and when Benson didn't reply, he continued. "The man that we really wanted wasn't even there. So we're going to have to go though this same shit again someday, and you can bet your ass on it!"

Finally Benson nodded his head in agreement. "That's for sure," he answered slowly. "If his damn followers wouldn't give up, you can damn well believe, Ryan, that whenever we catch up with Kenyatta he won't take the easy way out. No, the bastard will hold court in the streets," Benson stated, taking a sip from his cup. "But that will be one Black sonofabitch I'll be glad to see laying out on his back."

Suddenly there was a soft knock on their door. Ryan called out and a young white policewoman came through the door. She stopped right at the entrance and delivered her message. "The captain would like to see both of you in his office as soon as possible," she said, then backed out of the room.

"I knew it," Ryan said as he picked up his cup and blew in it before tipping it up and draining all of the contents. He set the empty cup down with a bang. "You make coffee like my fuckin' dog shits. It stinks."

Benson laughed as he set his cup down half full. "Well, in a second you won't have to worry about it. Or rather, you might be wishin' it had been poison before the captain gets through with our ass."

"It can't be that bad," Ryan replied. "In fact, I can't think of any reason for him to start chewing our asses out. Maybe he wants to pat us on the back for a good job done. Hell, if it hadn't been for us, we wouldn't have busted up the farmhouse."

"Yeah," Benson answered sarcastically. "We should get a medal of some kind for our work there. Shit, it ain't every day that our fellow officers get a chance to shoot the shit out of some broads!"

Ryan stopped at the door and stared at his partner. "You had better shake that fuckin' mood before we get in his office, Ben. I hate to see you taking this shit so hard, man. I think we were fortunate myself. Just stop and think, every damn cop that has been ambushed in the past has been revenged today. There's no doubt in my mind about it. Those crazy bastards that got their shit blown out for them today got what they had coming, and there's no two ways about it. For the past six months the poor bastards driving around on their fucking beat have been scared as hell to answer half the calls they get. And why? Because

Kenyatta's goddamn gang has been ambushing them! So don't feel sorry for them, Ben. Just be glad we got to most of them before they killed some more of us!"

Benson had to agree with what his partner said. He fell silent and led the way to Captain Davidson's office. They knocked softly and walked in, as the captain's loud voice came roaring at them through the door. The stout, graying officer stared at his two best detectives over his horn-rimmed glasses. The captain felt a touch of pride. These were the best detectives in homicide, but he wasn't going to let them know it.

There were three other men sitting around the small office. Captain Davidson quickly introduced all of the men to each other. "These gentlemen are with the federal government, and they would like for me to loan you two bums out to them," the captain stated, then added, "It seems as if you two guys know more about this fuckin' madman Kenyatta than anybody else in the country. So we are putting you on the case. Wherever Kenyatta goes, you boys will follow. Right now, they have hijacked an airplane, and from last report it was going down on the Nevada desert. You two will be flying out with special orders to work with whatever law enforcement branch that you need."

The two partners glanced at each other in surprise. This was truly something they hadn't expected. Before they could get over their surprise, Captain Davidson spoke up again.

"There's a special airplane waiting for you two at the airport. I expect you to go home and pack whatever you think you might need, and then get out to the airport within the next hour." He hesitated, then held out his hand. "Good luck to both of you. I just hope like hell you can break this damn case wide open and get it over with."

When the two officers walked back out of their captain's office, they were stunned. But they didn't waste any time. Each man took a different car with a driver to their homes. Within minutes, both men were packed. Benson kissed his wife good-bye and left, not realizing how long it would be before the trail of Kenyatta would end.

6

KENYATTA COUNTED HIS people as they came down the ladder. At the start he had had five experienced men. Each man had his own woman—a woman who had been trained in the art of death. Each one had been out on some kind of job that took nerve and a willing trigger finger. At least two of the women had killed before, so Kenyatta knew what kind of people he had chosen to take along with him. Now there were only three men who were able to withstand hardship. Red, because of his injury, was marked off. He had to be taken care of until he was back on his feet.

"Everybody is ready, honey," Betty called out, her voice carried across the now windy desert. Kenyatta could feel the change in the weather. As he started to walk toward the motorcycle that he would be riding, he thanked his lucky stars that none of the remaining women were hurt. Ann was dead, but since her man had been killed it was best that she had also gotten hit instead of one of the other women. They were still coupled up, and from the way he looked at it, that was just fine. Each man had the woman of his choice, so there was no reason why there should be any problems brought about over women.

Kenyatta glanced around at the couples on the bikes. There were six bikes so that came out right. Yet they still had a problem. With Red hurt, he wondered if Red's woman, Arlene, would be able to handle him on the motorcycle.

"Arlene," Kenyatta called out, "have you much experience bike riding?"

The slim brown-skinned woman shook her head. "Not much, Ken," she replied. "I've only rode by myself a couple of times. You remember, when that brother, what's his name, came out to the farm with the bike he had bought and stayed a few days. Well," she continued, "I got a chance to ride one by myself without havin' to ride behind some man."

Kenyatta laughed at her remark while his busy mind worked over the problem. He stared at the two white girls who were now on a bike together. The black-haired one was sitting on the driver's seat.

"You, Red," he yelled out at the redheaded woman who had "volunteered" his information, "are you a pretty good bike rider?"

The woman hesitated for a minute. "Well, I've been riding motorcycles for over five years now," she answered slowly.

"That ain't what the man asked you," Betty said, revealing the hatred she held for the white woman.

Kenyatta took a sharp look at his woman. She wasn't really herself, or so it seemed to him. He decided he would watch Betty kind of closely while the white women were their prisoners. Even though he didn't have any lost love for the two white women, he had given the redhead his promise that nothing would happen to her if she kept her head and didn't try anything smart.

"Well," the redheaded woman began, "Joan here is a tyro at bike riding," she stated, speaking of the black-haired girl.

Resorting to the snap judgments he was used to making, Kenyatta made his mind up at once. "Okay, we'll do it this way, then. Arlene, you give up your bike and go over and get behind that black-haired girl. Red, you get off that bike you're on and climb aboard the one with my hurt friend. I'm holding you responsible for him, so I don't want to see him topple off, you dig?"

"I understand," the white woman answered, then, fighting down her fear, added, "But your friend is hurt, and I'm not strong enough to ride with one hand and hold him with the other. He's hurt and he's going to have to hold on to me some kind of way. There should be some rough ground we're going to ride over, and since it's getting dark, none of us will be able to see too far ahead."

"Uh huh," Kenyatta answered as he sweated over the problem. He got back off the motorcycle where he had climbed on behind Betty. Kenyatta approached the white girl and the wounded man. "Red," he began, "first of all what the hell is your name? Since both of you are called Red I better get a better system of reaching either of you."

"Oh," she answered, surprised. "My name is Carol." As Kenyatta came up to them, she got her first good look at him up close and couldn't help admitting to herself that he was handsome in a dark sort of way. It surprised her, because it was one of the first times she had ever looked at a Black man in that way. Usually, the Black men who came into her company were servants or working as waiters or doormen. She seldom gave a second look to those kinds. They were below her, or so she felt. It was as though God had put them on earth just to function as undercover slaves. The crowd she ran around with took them for just that. Well paid slaves, and sometimes not that well paid.

"Red," he said, and put his arm on his friend's shoulder, "I see you are holding up pretty good." As Kenyatta talked he noticed the bandages the doctor had put over the wound. The doc had done a good job as far as he could tell. With the drugs in him, Red seemed to be in damn good shape for a man who had been hit in the shoulder, a wound that could turn out any kind of way.

"Yeah, baby," Red answered, the drugs making him feel much better. "I think I can hold my own, man."

"Uh huh," Kenyatta replied, seeing the slightly dazed look in his friend's eyes. The man was heavily drugged, there was no doubt about that. Kenyatta examined the motorcycle closely. It was too small for three people to ride. For that matter, none of the bikes were quite large enough for that.

"Look, Red," Kenyatta began, "we ain't got that far to go, but I don't want you falling off. Now, let me see. You used to ride a bike yourself, didn't you, Red?"

The short, light-skinned Negro answered slowly, his words coming out clearly. Still there was that hint of the man being high. "Yeah, Ken, you remember, at one time I was a bike freak. I was going to join one of them clubs before I got hooked up with you, man."

"Yeah, I remember, but I'm wonderin' if you've got the strength to ride, while she sits behind you and holds you up."

"I don't know," Red answered truthfully. "I feel cool, you know, for a man just being shot, but I ain't crazy. I know it's the morphine the doc gave me. The wound don't hurt, if I don't put no pressure on it, but trying to steer, or just hold one of these motherfuckers down might be more than I can manage."

"You're right," Kenyatta answered quickly, seeing the weakness in his idea at once. He started to get on the bike and ride it himself, but instantly remembered Betty's insane hatred for the white women and decided against it. The redheaded white woman wouldn't stand a chance if he ordered her up behind Betty. Before they reached the ranch Betty would have found some reason for killing the white girl. That much he was sure of.

"Goddamn, man, what the fuck are we goin' to do? Sit out here on the goddamn desert and freeze our ass off?" Eddie-Bee demanded.

The words the man used didn't upset Kenyatta, but the tone of voice sure as hell did. Kenyatta turned on Eddie-Bee quickly. His eyes turned to mere slits as his anger soared.

"What man? Just what the fuck did you say? Or rather, who the fuck were you talkin' to?" Kenyatta asked hotly.

"Hold on, brother," Eddie-Bee said quickly as he began to shake. "I didn't mean no harm, Kenyatta, I was just wondering, that's all."

"Well, don't wonder no goddamn more! You comprehend?" There was a deadliness about him that no one missed even though it was now too dark to see his face clearly.

"Yeah, Ken, yeah man, I dig. I didn't mean no harm though."

Kenyatta turned his back on the man and wished that it had been Eddie-Bee's little whining ass who had got killed instead of his mellow man Zeke. The hurt of Zeke's killing hadn't set in yet with him, only because he hadn't had time to slow down and think about it. But he knew he would miss the tall Black man. He and Zeke had gone through a lot of things together.

"Well," Kenyatta began, speaking so everybody could hear, "we ain't got much choice. Red, wrap your arms around the woman's waist. Let me see how good you can hold on."

When Red attempted to use the right arm, a groan of pain escaped from him. "Goddamn!" Red cursed. He could only manage to get one arm around the woman.

Kenyatta almost pulled his pistol to knock the man out, but just as instantly disregarded the fleeting idea. If Red fell off the bike he would more than likely knock himself out, or die. Either way, it would benefit the small group of fleeing Blacks. The way Red was now, he was causing them more problems than they could afford.

"Okay, Red," Kenyatta stated. "It's goin' have to be like this. You're strong as hell, Red, we ain't got no doubts about that, so now is one of the times you're going to have to really prove it to us. I remember the way you used to lift all that iron back at the farm, impressing the women with your muscles. So now is the time to see if all that weightlifting paid off. I want you to get a good hold on her with your good arm." Kenyatta watched closely as Red did as he ordered. "That's right," Kenyatta continued, "Hug that white ass boy! I mean hug it like you had your dick stuck up into that white ass and she was tryin' to get away from all that Black dick!"

Red grinned at his leader's words and smiled when he felt the woman he held tighten up. "I dig what you mean, Ken," he replied. "Shit, man, she got a soft ass at that!"

"Maybe I should have stayed over there," Arlene called out when she heard Red's words. The fresh air and quiet summer night made words carry a long way on the desert.

Inside the airplane, people glanced out the windows, trying to figure out what the hell was going on. They could see the lights of the motorcycles in a circle and not going anywhere. The white man Kenyatta had sent up into the plane had already told a group of them about the dude ranch, so they knew the destination of the small group of militant Blacks. Some more of the passengers had gone up front and found the dead pilots and the damaged radio. Already some of the passengers were discussing their plight and how and what they could do about it.

Back on the ground Kenyatta had decided it

was time to be getting on. "Carol," he said, "what's your friend's name?"

Carol adjusted herself on the seat, trying to help the man behind her make himself comfortable. "That's Joan," she replied.

"Fine," Kenyatta answered, then started back to his own bike. He beckoned for Betty to get off, then he quickly took the driver's seat. He started the motorcycle with a roar, waited until Betty got behind him, then rode over to where Joan sat on her bike with Arlene behind her.

"Joan," he began, "I want you to lead off. Now girl, I ain't goin' tell you but one time. No tricks. Don't take us the long way either. Just ride like you got Godgiven sense and everything will be all right. If you come up with some trick and get rid of Arlene, who's behind you, I'll drop my woman off and ride your ass down, do you understand?" He waited a second until the woman nodded her head in understanding, then waved to the others.

Suddenly the night was shattered with the loud sound of the motorcycles starting up all at once. Inside the airplane, the stranded passengers pressed their faces against the windows trying to see the departure of the motorcycles. From where they were they could see the lights of the bikes as they moved into what looked like a ragged single file and moved off across the endless desert. Many of the passengers sighed a sigh of relief when they saw this. They were all happy to see the departure of the murdering Blacks.

"Jesus Christ," one of the passengers called out, "I think I'm so happy to see those crazy fuckers leave, it's like, I don't know, maybe what a drowning man must feel when he finds himself coming up for help and someone has an arm around his waist!"

A few people agreed with him. Another man began to complain. "I don't know what the hell you're happy about! Here we are stuck out here on the desert with two dead pilots on our hands, maybe not enough water to last us another day, and you're happy?"

"You're damn right I'm happy," the man replied. "This guy here," he said, pointing to the man who had been sent aboard by Kenyatta, "tells us there's a ranch a few miles away, so we sure in the hell won't die of thirst out here!"

The second man laughed coldly. "I thought you were just thanking God that you had seen the last of those killers. Now you turn around and say you want to go running over the hill and catch up with them!" His brutal laugh killed the dreams of many of the people aboard who had been thinking in the same vein.

But the man who had spoken first didn't back off. "You better damn well bet I'm planning on going over that hill. All you have to do is use a little common sense. Those people who had just left here are on the run, so you can bet your ass they won't let any grass grow under their fuckin' feet. By the time we walk across this desert with some of the older people on this plane in tow they will have had plenty time to bring death and destruction to the people on the ranch."

The slim white man who was sent aboard spoke up. His face was set in a look of horror. "You don't think they will hurt the people at the ranch, do you?"

Most of the passengers stared at the man as if he were a fool. One of the women passengers said coldly, "Are you sure you possess the sense to lead us to the ranch?"

The worried man missed the sarcasm behind her words as he said, "By God, my wife is back at the ranch! Jesus Christ, I've got to get out of here and get back and try and help her!" He started for the door.

Two of the nearest male passengers grabbed him and held him forcefully. "You fool, you!" one of them screamed to his face. "Just what in the hell do you think you could do even if you were there? Just look around you." He pointed at the bodies that were now lined up in a neat row in the aisles.

The other man who held his arm spoke up, "Don't worry, they don't seem to hurt women. If your wife is smart and keeps her head, they won't bother her." He pointed at the body of a dead man. "If it hadn't been for that silly bastard there, I doubt if any bodies would be down there. He started the goddamn gun fight, and this is what it led to."

His words brought argument from some of the other passengers who were inclined to put all the blame on the militant Blacks. But the man held on firmly to his belief. They continued to argue on into the night, while trying to make up their minds when to leave the airplane. None of them wanted to leave too soon, and by some odd chance of fate catch up with the Black group. Some of the passengers argued that it would be best to wait until morning. Others claimed that by morning it would be too hot for some of the older passengers to walk. The heat would kill them before they got fifty feet.

There were over ten people on board who were in their seventies and eighties, while a few more were nearing the age of retirement. The stewardess checked the water supply and informed them that there was not enough to last more than one day. After much quarreling it was decided that fifteen of the youngest men aboard would go for help. The number was reached as a way to save on some of the water. The young men could go without drinking since it wasn't but a five mile walk, while the older people would just sit on the airplane and wait until help came. There was food enough to hold them, and soft drinks that would take the place of water. The only problem facing them was on the time to depart. None of them wanted to arrive at the ranch too soon. They wanted to give the Blacks plenty of time to get there and do whatever they were going to do. With that thought in all their minds, they settled down to wait. After much discussion, they decided that two o'clock in the morning would be a good time for them to start walking. By the time they reached the ranch it would be light enough for them to see, and if they saw the Blacks still around, all they would have to do would be turn around and come back toward the plane. Few of them believed the Blacks would hurt them once they saw that they didn't intend to give them any trouble. After a little more discussion, they decided to insure their well being by taking the only Black man on the airplane along. They could use him for a message carrier, since it had been made clear that the Blacks wouldn't hurt the other Blacks if they would only stay the hell out of the way.

The only Black man on the plane argued for quite a while that he meant to stay out of their way. He wanted to stay with the plane and wait for help. But after much discussion he was finally talked into leaving with the other able-bodied men.

7

KENYATTA KEPT HIS front wheel only a foot behind Joan's motorcycle. The roar of the bikes
was loud but none of the riders paid any attention
to it. Most of them wondered what awaited them
at the ranch. But Kenyatta wasn't worried about
the ranch. He was thinking much further ahead
than that. If he could only reach Los Angeles he
could make a connection with other members of
his gang. He had people living in Los Angeles,
members who had moved away from the Motor
City but who stayed hip to the organization. Some
had left because it became too hot for them to
stay. These were the ones who were dedicated.

Joan was taking her time and trying to pick out
the smoothest route through the darkened sand
hills. The night was pitch black and the riders

were having trouble making out the bikes in front of them. Kenyatta noticed that Joan slowed her speed down slightly. He took the opportunity to slow a little and move behind Carol and Red. He noticed that Red was swaying. He couldn't tell if it was from the motion of the bike, or because the wounded man was having a hard time holding on. Suddenly it happened. It seemed as if they hit a small ridge and the bike in front of them bounced and Red toppled off.

Before Kenyatta could react his motorcycle hit the same ridge, and he had a hard time bringing the bike back under control. By the time he did, he smashed into the back of Carol's bike. She had stopped the moment Red fell off.

Betty let out a loud curse and jumped from the back of the motorcycle. Kenyatta had just enough time to drop the bike and grab at his woman as she fumbled with the shoulder holster she had put on. Her magnum hung up on her as she snatched wildly at it. If she had taken her time, she would have been able to bring it out before Kenyatta reached her, but as it was he was able to knock the gun spinning from her hand. She cursed loudly, but now he was aroused. His temper flared and without hesitation he brought up his right hand and slapped her viciously across the mouth. Before she could react, he had slapped her again.

"Goddamn it, bitch," he roared as the other bikes came to skidding stops around them. "I don't know what the fuck has got into you, but you had better get it out of your system!"

"What's happenin'?" Jug called out as be climbed down off his motorcycle.

"This ignorant bitch here is tryin' her goddamn best to fuck everything up," Kenyatta yelled as he went over to Red's aid. Red lay in the sand where he had fallen, not moving.

Carol, after putting her kickstand down, ran back from her bike and knelt down beside the wounded man. He groaned as she lifted his head to her lap. "It looks as if his wound has burst open," she said as she held him tenderly in her arms.

Betty walked slowly up to the kneeling group. "I don't think that was really called for, daddy," she said as she held the side of her face.

"You don't huh!" Kenyatta yelled harshly at her, "Well, ignorant ass bitch, try this on for size! First of all, I done told you to leave this damn woman alone. If she gets out of line, I'm quite able to take care of her. But no, you goin' go ahead and act as if I ain't said nothing and blow the woman's damn brains out, and what the kicker is, you was going to do it for nothing. Even after. . . ."

"I wasn't going to do it for nothing," Betty said quickly, interrupting Kenyatta. "You saw the way she knocked Red off that bike, honey! I know you did! You couldn't possibly have missed it."

For a second, Kenyatta was so mad that he couldn't reply. When he regained some sort of control he stated, "What the hell are you talking about, woman? You better damn well believe I saw what happened. I saw her slow her bike down as she tried to pick the best route, and also I saw what happened when she hit that fuckin' ridge. We damn near flipped over ourselves when we hit it right behind her, so how the hell can you hold her responsible for that?" Before she could say anything else, Kenyatta continued, "It's so damn dark out here, I'm surprised she hasn't hit a deep ridge before this. But regardless of that shit, Betty, I've told you to be cool, yet you wanted to shoot this woman, even though we need the hell out of her services. And," he added, as he warmed up to his subject, "in your stupidity you would put everybody's life in more danger than it already is by warning the people at the ranch that somebody near at hand has a gun. Common sense would tell you that sound travels like hell out here, but you don't give a shit. Naw, hell no! It don't make you no difference one way or the other, just as long as you get your pound of flesh, I guess."

"It wasn't like that, daddy, really," Betty pleaded. "I thought she had intentionally hit that huge bump and caused Red to fall off. So without thinkin', I was goin' fix her smart white ass for her!" Betty dropped her head in shame; she wasn't used to Kenyatta scolding her, and in front of other people it was damn near unheard of. She knew at once that she had really been out of step for her man to come down on her so hard. Betty bit her lip until the blood ran, as she tried to hold back the tears of shame. But no matter what she did, she couldn't control them. She glanced around and was thankful it was so dark. She prayed that no one had noticed. She turned her back on the crowd and walked back to her motorcycle.

For a brief instant, Kenyatta almost called her back as he remembered the strong pills the doctor had given them for Red. But pills wouldn't do any good at the moment, he reflected. Red was out cold.

"Goddamn, Ken," Jug said as he stepped up beside Kenyatta. "Looks like Red is going to cause us one hell of a problem. If he don't pull himself together, I don't know what we goin' work out of when we get off this desert and in a city. Shit, people will be noticing us as it is. It's so many of us that we can't help but to draw attention wherever we go."

"Uh huh," Kenyatta answered with his stock reply. "What you say makes sense, Jug, but we ain't got to worry about that problem until we reach a city. Right now, we're over a hundred miles away from one." Without really meaning to, Kenyatta had checked Jug, and did it coldly and harshly. His words had been like razor cuts, the tone of his voice revealing his anger.

Jug realized at once that he had brought up a sore point with his leader and quickly made his exit. Following Betty's example, he walked back to the bike he had ridden and climbed up on the seat and made himself comfortable. Kenyatta didn't want to face the facts, he reflected, as he thought about the matter. Red was hurt and holding them back. The best thing they could do would be to put a bullet in Red's head and keep on pushing. If they didn't, Red was going to be their downfall. Jug believed himself to be a dedicated member of the organization, but he couldn't see himself getting busted because one of the members was hurt and the rest of them were too chicken-hearted to put him out of their way. Well, he decided, he'd play it by ear from here on out, but he wasn't planning on letting Red be the cause of his going to prison for life. He didn't try and fool himself. He knew that if they got busted, life in prison was what every one of them faced. Even the women. Not even the women would get out from under it with less than all day in prison.

Working on him quietly, Carol was still able to see everything that went down. She also realized that the tall Black man beside her had saved her life. A sensation that was more like a thrill ran through her when Kenyatta knelt down beside her. Just his nearness made her feel different. The man who she held in her lap didn't move her whatsoever, but the Black man next to her was something else. She wondered what would it be like to lie in those Black arms and let him hold her tightly with the bulging muscles that she couldn't help but notice. The man is a killer, she told herself, but it didn't do any good. For the first time in her life she wanted a Black man. Now she knew why the white women she had seen with black men did what they did. Before, she had always looked down her nose at them. But now, she knew beyond a shadow of a doubt why. Just the thought of him holding her was enough for her to feel her legs getting wet. She could feel her cunt twitching in desire. It was as though that part of her had a mind of its own. She let out a groan that Kenyatta mistook for a sound from Red.

"So he's coming around, huh?" Kenyatta asked quietly, his deep voice sounding manly in her ear.

"No, no, not really," Carol managed to say. "Maybe it would be better if he stayed unconscious until we reached the ranch. It's just over the next sand dune," she stated in a husky voice. She turned and brushed against him as she pointed out the sand dune they would have to cross.

Kenyatta couldn't help but inhale the sweet smelling perfume she wore. It had a fragrance to it that was enticing. He found himself drawn to her. She was the first white woman in his life that he had ever been curious about. All his life he had despised white people, and especially Black men with white women. He found his new attraction strange and baffling. It wasn't like him, and to want a white woman sexually was really against his nature. But here he was hoping she would lean against him again.

When she didn't, he pretended to bend down

KENYATTA'S ESCAPE

and hold Red's head, but he let his arm brush against her tits. He heard a tiny gasp from her and didn't know if it was from fear or from the dislike of having a Black man touch her. The second thought added anger to his reasoning and he made up his mind that he would surely touch her again when the opportunity presented itself. Then he would find out if she disliked a Black touching her so much that she had to moan.

After a few more minutes of staying bent down over Red, Kenyatta realized that the man wasn't going to wake up for a while. He glanced up at the small crowd that was around them. "Hey, no wonder the guy can't come around. You get back to your bikes. That way he can get some air. As it is, with everybody crowded around, the man probably can't get his proper air."

When Carol started to stand up, he put his hand on her arm and detained her. He waited until everybody had left except for Red's woman, then he beckoned for her to kneel down.

As Arlene dropped to her knees beside her man, Kenyatta stood up. He stepped behind Carol and raised her to her feet by her elbows. It was too dark for the rest of the group to see what he was doing, and Arlene was too busy fussing over her man to care.

Using her elbows, he pulled Carol to her feet. Before he collected his wits about him and did what he wanted to do with her, she did it herself. When she came up she leaned back against him, which was just what he was planning on forcing her to do. She seemed to lose her balance and mumbled something about her feet having gone to sleep.

Kenyatta held her close and smelled the top of her head. Her rather large ass rested right on his penis as he held her tightly in his arms. He could feel his manhood growing larger as it became harder. He pressed himself up between her buttocks as though his prick could bust through his pants and split open her white shorts. He felt like it could, as he wondered if his dick had ever gotten that hard before. Her breathing became ragged as she seemed to sag in his arms. For a brief moment, he just stood still and slowly ground his huge penis against her. It took all the will power Kenyatta possessed to break the spell. Finally, he pushed her away from his embrace. "Your husband will get one hell of a surprise when all of us arrive back at the ranch, won't he?"

Her laughter rang out sharply. Then she said loud enough for all the group to hear, "My husband got his surprise when he climbed aboard the airplane. The blond-headed one was him."

Kenyatta stared at the woman, shocked by her coldness. She had never bothered to inquire from any of them as to whether or not her man was dead. Yes, she had heard the two shots like everybody else on the ground, but that didn't mean that her husband was dead. He might have been wounded. Maybe the shots hadn't been meant for him. She had no way of knowing and hadn't bothered to ask.

"Aren't you curious about whether or not he's alive?" Kenyatta asked.

"No!" she answered truthfully enough. "From the way your people killed everybody else, I shouldn't think a pig-headed man like my husband would have had enough sense to keep himself from getting killed. He would have to make some kind of stupid display or it wouldn't be him. Since I heard the gunshots as soon as he entered the airplane, I took it for granted that he tried to be the hero and got his reward. Am I right?"

She waited patiently for his answer. If he had said anything other than what she hoped to hear, Carol would have been disappointed. These people had lifted a burden off her back, plus made her the owner of the ranch. Now all she had to do was survive and she would be well off the rest of her life.

"Yes, you're definitely right about that. Your husband didn't waste any time gettin' himself killed," Kenyatta replied, as he tried to study the woman in the dark. She was a cold broad, that was one thing he was sure of. Here her husband was just killed, yet she was more than willing to go to bed with the man who was really responsible for her husband's death. Maybe, he decided, she hated her man just that much.

Kenyatta called out to Betty. "Honey, you ride the bike, I'm going with this wood. When she pulls up in the yard I'm going to be so close to her that if she breathes wrong I'll know about it." Kenyatta realized that the excuse he gave for riding with Carol was a long way from the real. He wanted to hold that white flesh in his arms once again, and he knew that before the night was out, he was going to bed her down, whether Betty liked it or not.

Carol walked slowly toward her bike. They had to pass Betty, and she could feel the other woman's hatred for her as she went past. Betty's eyes looked as if they were glowing in the dark, she was so angry. But there was nothing she could do about it. Kenyatta had given the order, and that was that. She snatched the bike up that she was supposed to ride and started the motor. Betty revved the motorcycle three or four times as she waited for the white woman and her man to get on the bike in front of her. Betty felt for her weapon, then remembered that Kenyatta had taken it from her.

"Honey," Betty called out in the dark, "don't you think I should have my weapon back now? Something might jump off at the ranch and I'll be needin' it, and you might not have the time to toss it to me." Betty waited for him to hand her the gun.

At first, Kenyatta started to give her the gun, but on second thought he decided to hold it. "Naw, ain't nothing goin' go wrong at the ranch, woman, unless I give you the gun and you go shootin' it off at the wrong time. I think the best thing I can do is hold on to it until we have a littl' talk. You been gettin' beside yourself, Betty, and it seems as if the time has come for me to put a littl' restraint on you."

Each word that came out of his mouth was like a slap in the face. At first she couldn't believe it. Then she just sat on the bike dumbfounded until he finished speaking. Before she could even plead, he had moved onto another subject.

"Arlene," Kenyatta called out, "honey, I want you to stay here with Red until we get to the ranch. Then I'm going to send somebody back with one of them dune buggies. That away, he won't be jarred to death, and we won't have to worry about busting his wound open. I couldn't leave him back at the plane, but now we're far enough ahead of the people from the plane so you don't have any worry. The ranch is just over the next hill, so it shouldn't take more than twenty or thirty minutes before we get back." Suddenly Kenyatta turned on Betty. "You park that bike and stay and keep her company. Here," he said and reached in his belt and removed the gun from under it. "You make damn sure you don't shoot this thing unless you have to. Don't fire for any reason unless you believe we have reached the ranch."

Kenyatta stood beside the bike and stared out into the darkness. He couldn't really see the people he talked to, nor could they see him, but his voice carried the authority they were used to hearing.

"Jug, pull your bike up here beside me. When we hit that ranch yard, I want you right next to me." Everyone listening couldn't help but to believe that that was the only thing Kenyatta had on his mind—to take the ranch without losing any more of his people.

Betty, listening in the dark, felt ashamed. She had let her man down with her silly jealousy. Here he was worried about how to knock off the ranch house, and all she could think about was killing the white woman because she believed the white woman wanted her man. In all the years she had known Kenyatta she had never known him to even glance back at a white woman, so why should she come up with her silly jealousy? Even as dark as I am, Betty reflected, people would be able to see me blush. She was sure her face was lit up with shame. She thanked her gods for blessing her with the darkness of night, so that no one could see her shame.

"Okay, honey," Betty said softly, "but you be sure to be careful, hear," she called out.

As Kenyatta glanced in the darkness toward where his woman was supposed to be, he felt a stab of shame. This was the first time he had ever cheated on her, and he wasn't proud of himself for doing it. "Don't worry, baby," he called back, "and I'll be sending that dune buggy for you as soon as we've got everything taken care of down there, hear?"

Before she could answer, he ordered Carol to start the motor up. Whatever Betty said went unheard, because the roar of Carol's motorcycle drowned out her voice.

Kenyatta sat up close on the seat, causing Carol to almost sit in his lap. She pulled away with a jerk, then they were on their way across the sand. As she drove, Kenyatta held her tightly in his arms. He reached around and felt for the front of the very brief shorts she wore. His inquiring fingers found the buttons and he quickly unbuttoned them. He ran his gnarled fingers around inside her panties and was surprised at the softness of the hairs on Carol's pussy. It was the first time he had ever felt a white woman and it came as a shock. The hair felt like soft silk to him. He inserted his finger inside of her, and Carol let out a groan and damn near let the motorcycle get out of control. She couldn't stand his finger up inside her. It was too much.

Jug was driving his bike right behind them and wondered what the hell was going on. As soon as they topped the hill, Kenyatta pulled his hand away and glared seriously down at the sleeping ranch house. There were only a few lights on.

Kenyatta yelled in Carol's ear, "Do you think everybody down there is asleep?"

At first she shook her head, then she yelled over the noise of the motor. "No way! They saw the plane come down and decided to wait until we got back to find out what happened."

As they came roaring down the hill, her words came true. The front door of the ranch house opened and two men and three women came rushing out into the yard. They didn't really notice that the riders were different until Carol pulled up in front of them and Kenyatta climbed down off the back of her bike. Before the people could react, the other bikes had surrounded them.

As the bikes pulled to a stop, guns suddenly appeared in the hands of most of the riders. "What the hell goes on here, Carol?" a short, gray-haired man yelled out.

"Oh, Bill," Joan cried as she leaped from her bike and ran to the man, "these awful people killed Tony and the rest of them."

Bill held Joan in his arms, stroking her hair. "Oh," he said, "these must be the people they were talking about on the news who hijacked an airplane in Michigan!"

"That's right, Jack!" Eddie-Bee said as he came forward, waving his gun. "Ken," Eddie-Bee called out, "what we goin' do with 'em? Should we kill 'em and get them out of the fuckin' way or take them back into the house and tie them up?"

"Please, please," Carol begged, "don't kill them. They won't give you any trouble, isn't that right, Bill?" She was begging for their lives.

The other white man suddenly raised his hands in the air. "Please," he begged, "I won't give you any trouble whatsoever, just let me live. I promise, you won't even know I'm around."

Kenyatta glanced at the long-haired younger man. He believed that the man meant what he said. "Okay, buddy boy," Kenyatta replied, "I'm going to give all of you a chance. But whoever fucks up won't have to worry about seconds. Bring them on in the house. Carol, how many servants are there on the place? I mean ranch hands and cooks, everybody."

Carol shook her head. "There's nobody here but us. We do our own cooking and there's enough of us women so that it's not a hassle for any of us. The men do whatever saddling needs to be done if anybody should want to horseback ride, but we don't ride enough to keep any hired help. There is one man who takes care of the horses, but when we are here, he is allowed to go into town and stay. When he sees us leave, or we call him and let him know that we are leaving, then he comes back out here and stays until we come back down for another vacation."

Before anybody else could say anything, one of the women who had run out into the yard screamed out, "Where's Jim? Where the hell is my husband?"

"Don't worry, June, he'll be home soon," Joan replied. "They left him with the other people on the airplane."

Now that the woman had brought out the question, the other two women began to ask about their men. Kenyatta cut them off quickly, not allowing anyone to tell them that their men had been killed.

"Jug," Kenyatta called out, "get these fuckin' people inside the house and see to it that they are tied up tight. This ain't no question and answer period, so keep your fuckin' mouths closed. That is, if you want to live to see another day," Kenyatta added coldly.

Before the women had time to think, Jug began to usher them toward the house. The men moved along meekly enough so that there was no problem. Kenyatta watched from beside the motorcycle. He turned to the few of his people that remained in the yard. "The rest of you go into the house and see that everything stays under control. I'll be back inside in a few minutes. I'm going to check out the dune buggies so that Red can get picked up."

Kenyatta watched them walk toward the house slowly. He waited until everybody was inside, then he spoke to Carol. "Over there at the horse stable, what do you keep inside there, other than the horses?"

Without hesitation, Carol spoke up. "Well, we have a place for the motorcycles there, and also one for the dune buggies."

"Good," Kenyatta replied. "Let's go over and check out the dune buggies." Without waiting for her, he turned his back and started walking in that direction. In seconds, the tall, attractive white woman had caught up with him. He took her arm, and by the time they had reached the stable his arm was all the way around her slim waist. He pulled her close, feeling her tremble as he held her tightly in his arms. The closer he held her, the sharper her breath became. Kenyatta kicked the barn door open and pulled her inside. The stable was well kept, each stall was clean, and there was not a strong odor of horse shit. It might have been because there were only four horses in the stable. The remaining room had been converted, into a garage for the dune buggies and motorcycles.

They walked slowly down the center of the stable, neither one saying anything. Kenyatta searched for the ideal place. Suddenly at the rear of the stable he found what he was looking for. There was a pile of freshly cut hay. He led Carol over to the hay and both of them fell down into it. Kenyatta's arms quickly folded around her. He held her tightly, kissing her slowly. Without wasting any time, he began to remove her shorts. She murmured something about stopping, but he paid no heed. In seconds, she was lying back in the hay naked.

Kenyatta took his time and kissed her breasts, then he let his tongue run down over her narrow ribcage. She began to make funny noises deep down in her throat.

As he slowly played with her, building up the tension inside her, Kenyatta could feel his manhood slowly swelling inside his pants. Soon his penis was as hard as a rock. He removed his pants quickly and knelt down between the woman's legs. Carol opened them widely as she put her arm across her face, almost as though afraid to look. Suddenly she could feel his weight on top of her as he stretched out on her prone body.

At first she hadn't meant to make any noise, but as she felt him begin to penetrate her, she cried out in pain. "Please," she cried, "I don't think I can take you. It's too large!"

At the sound of her voice, Kenyatta only laughed. He knew he was extra large, and he also knew he was going to enjoy it. Her sharp cries of pain quickly reversed themselves until she was moaning from pleasure. It wasn't long before Kenyatta found himself caught up in the act. He was soaring higher and higher from a feeling of euphoria. Soon, he couldn't contain himself and he exploded inside of her. Her scream of contentment rang out alongside of his own. They held each other in a bear hug as Kenyatta found himself going off inside of her again and again.

A few minutes later, after they had cleaned themselves up, Carol found herself staring at the tall Black man in fascination. Never before in her life had a man made her feel the way he had just done. It was something out of a dream. She had never believed it could be true. Sex to her had become a weapon that she used on the men who came into her life. Now she found herself on the other side of the coin. As she stood up she could feel her legs shaking.

"Hey," Kenyatta called out from over by the parked dune buggies that he was closely examining. "I believe this should do the trick," he said, his mind back on business. "Where do you keep the keys for these toys?"

"You don't have to worry about a key," Carol answered, as she walked over to him. She found herself fighting down the urge to put her hands on the tall man. "The switches on all the dune buggies have been fixed so that they run without keys."

"Good," he replied and climbed in. "Open up the barn door for me."

She stared at him closely for a second. It seemed as if he had completely forgotten about the incident between them. She couldn't believe he had put it out of his memory that fast.

Kenyatta watched her walk slowly back to the door and begin opening both of them. He had to shake his head. It had been quite a while since a woman had made him feel like that. Even though Betty was an excellent bed partner, they had been together so long that he knew each sound she was going to make before she ever made it. Something new never hurt, he reflected, then he smiled to himself. These white broads did have a little something going for them after all. As soon as both doors were open, he put the thought out of his mind and slipped the dune buggy into gear. He had a lot of things to take care of, and none of them could wait.

After backing out of the stable, Kenyatta beck-

oned for Carol. "Come along, baby, you had better show me the way back. I don't want to take
any chances on gettin' lost out there on this goddamn desert!"

She came over and climbed into the buggy.
Kenyatta started back out the way they came. The
only thing moving on the desert, it seemed, was
them. The stars blazed down brightly as the moon
shone silvery fingers all along the sand. The late
evening air was chilly. There was no top, only iron
bars welded over them. The large tires made it
easy driving through the sand, and in a matter of
minutes they were pulling up beside Betty, Arlene
and Red.

Kenyatta slowly climbed out of the buggy. "I
think it will be best if we lay him down across the
backseat. The rest of us can pile in some kind of
way in the front. At least out here we won't have
to worry about gettin' a ticket for riding four in
the front."

Neither of the two Black women smiled or
spoke as they got in. Betty rolled her eyes at the
white woman, but didn't make any more comments. Arlene helped Kenyatta settle Red in the
rear of the car, then found a place in the front.
They rode back to the ranch house in silence.
Kenyatta was deep in his personal thoughts, so he
paid no attention to the women.

Kenyatta pulled the dune buggy right up to the
front door of the ranch, then got out and called
for Jug. Jug came out the front door, his pistol in

his hand. When he saw who it was he holstered the gun and came down the short front steps.

Kenyatta lifted the unconscious man out of the buggy, then Jug grabbed Red's feet. Between them they managed to get the wounded man inside the ranch house. It was Kenyatta's first time inside the place, so he glanced around curiously. Instantly the realization went through his mind that the fuckin' broad was rich. From the expensive furniture that filled the large living room, it was obvious that someone had spent a lot of money on the place. The carpet on the floor was a deep purple, while expensive throw rugs crossed each other everywhere he looked. Paintings hung on the walls and the drapes were a rich velvet.

At the sight of all the white people tied up and laid out on the dining room floor, Kenyatta smiled. It had been well done. Even without them there the whites would have trouble getting themselves free from the sheets that had been torn into strips and used to tie them.

"Well done, Jug," Kenyatta said as he spoke to his friend.

Eddie-Bee came out of the kitchen carrying a jug of wine. "I got to give these peckerwoods credit," he said, his voice already becoming tangled from the drink. "These woods sure as hell know how to live. Ken, you ought to see the bar placed back near the inside swimming pool. Man, is it out of sight! Some of the kids want to take a swim!"

Kenyatta used the back of his hand to wipe his eyes. He knew he was becoming sleepy, but he blamed it on the short bout at sex. "I doubt if we're going to have that much fuckin' time, but if we do, they can go ahead and jump in the goddamn pool," he stated, then turned to Betty. "Honey, you better check out the food problem. We don't know when we'll find the time to eat again, so see to it that plenty of food is prepared." He then let himself down into an expensive armchair. "Damn, it sure in the hell feels good just to relax," he said, speaking to no one in particular.

What seemed like just a few minutes turned into an hour, then Kenyatta felt someone shaking him. He had fallen asleep in the chair. As soon as he was awake, his keen mind was clicking. He could hear splashing sounds coming from the rear of the ranch where some of his people were taking a swim.

"Here, daddy," Betty said, holding out a plate of fried chicken and mashed potatoes. "I would have awakened you sooner, but I know you needed some kind of rest."

He smiled up at her ruefully as he took the plate of food. His eyes went to the prisoners and he noticed instantly that while he had slept someone had tied Carol up. Kenyatta decided not to comment on it. He knew instantly who had been the one responsible for having the white woman tied.

Betty hadn't missed the glance he tossed in the

white woman's direction, and for the thousandth time, she wondered if Kenyatta had done anything with her. Her hatred rose suddenly, but she managed to conceal it as she smiled down at Kenyatta.

"You better try and get a little sleep yourself, Betty. We goin' be pullin' out of here pretty damn soon."

"Aw shit!" she exclaimed. "I was hoping we could hold up here for a couple of days."

Kenyatta glanced up at her suddenly. "You can't mean that?"

"Yes I do," she replied quickly, "and some of the other kids were hopin' the same thing. It's so nice here, we could have a wonderful time."

"Well I'll be damned!" Kenyatta stated, then laughed abruptly. "That's why ya have to have somebody lead you. If you thought for your fuckin' selves, you'd be lost. Here the police are going to be swarming all over this goddamn desert in another day, and ya want to lay out on this goddamn ranch and await them!" He raised his hand and waved her away. "Take that shit elsewhere," he stated and started eating his food.

As he ate, Kenyatta went over their problems. He knew the searchers would be out at daylight looking for the downed airplane, so before daylight he knew they would have to make the move. If they moved fast enough, they could escape the net that was drawing tight around them. But he would have to move very fast. He wanted to make some calls but knew whatever numbers he called would be traced by the police whenever they found out that his people had held up at the ranch. It wouldn't do to bring the heat down on the few remaining people in his organization, because he was sure the people back at his farmhouse had been busted. He wondered idly if they had put up any kind of fight, or had everybody surrendered as soon as they saw the law pulling up. Well, now sure in the hell wasn't the time to find out, he reasoned. Yet, he'd like to make contact with his people in Los Angeles. But again, the telephone would be traced and he'd be bringing down heat on them. Damn, he swore as he bit down on a drumstick, what the hell was he going to do? He listened to the sounds of glee coming from the pool and wondered how they could relax so damn easy.

"How about loosening up this damn sheet?" Carol called out to him.

He glanced over at her and got up. Kenyatta knelt down beside her and noticed at once that her hands had been tied extra tight. He frowned at the sight of her white, bloodless hands, then quickly released her from her bonds.

Carol stood up on shaky legs, "Thanks, I don't think I've ever been so glad to get out of something."

Kenyatta only nodded and walked back to his

chair. He beckoned for her to follow him. When she had seated herself across from him, he began to speak.

"Red," he said, "I'm going to need some information from you, and no bullshit!" He stared into her eyes, then continued. "We're going to have to leave your nice place, even though it seems as if quite a few of my members are havin' the ball of their lives." He waited until she smiled slightly, then added, "How many ways out of here are there?"

"Only one," she answered quickly. "You have to follow the road leading away from here until it reaches the main highway, which leads either toward Vegas or Los Angeles, depending on which way you turn."

"Suppose I turned right, which way would I be going?" Kenyatta asked, taking his time and studying the woman's face in front of him.

"Then you'd be on your way to Vegas," she replied quietly.

"Uh huh," he said as his mind went over his possibilities. "Tell me something, Carol. If we took all the transportation except the dune buggies, would you people be all right?"

She hesitated for a minute. "It would be a long ride," she stated, "but we could make it out with the buggies, or we could call on the telephone and have a private airplane pick us up."

"Yeah, I guess you could," he stated as he rubbed his chin. "Jug," Kenyatta called out sharply, then waited a few seconds until the man appeared. Jug was wearing a pair of short blue jeans with the legs cut out. He had been using them to swim in. Water dripped from his body onto the floor as he walked over to where Kenyatta sat.

"What's up, baby?" he inquired as he came up to the couple. For some reason, almost all the members were leaving Kenyatta alone.

"How's Red coming along?" Kenyatta asked.

Jug shook his head. "The guy has come to a few times, so we dumped some of them pills into him, and he's gone back to sleep." Jug hesitated, then added, "I don't know how he'll be when we start traveling, but so far he looks good." Jug raised his hands, then let them fall. "You dig where I'm coming from, Ken? The man ain't got no damn fever nor is he raving. None of that kind of shit. You never can tell about gunshots. Some guys go out of their mind from the pain and that kind of shit, but so far, Red seems to be holding up real good."

"Uh huh," Kenyatta replied, then added, "I want you to see to it that all the fuckin' telephones or any other form of communication that they have around here is destroyed. Not later, but right now. Get the rest of the group on the case also. Have them be sure and search for one of those private walkie-talkies or whatever they call them. Anything that they could reach the outside with, get rid of them."

"Yeah, my man, I dig where you're coming from,"

Jug answered. "But there might be an easier way than that," he added, waiting on Kenyatta's reply.

"Yeah, Jug, and what would that be?" Kenyatta asked quietly, already knowing what the answer would be.

"Well," Jug began, not really liking the frown his leader had on his face. For some reason, Kenyatta had taken a liking to the white girl. Jug was reluctant to speak in front of her. Fuck her, he said to himself, then patted the gun on his hip. "A few well placed bullets, Kenyatta, and these honkies won't be tellin' nobody which way we went."

Kenyatta glanced at the white woman and noticed that she was trembling visibly. He decided to quickly put her mind at rest. As Carol stared at the tall Black man who she had sex with, she realized that her life depended on his very next words. If he said die, they would all die. The whites lying in the dining room had overheard the conversation, and all of them waited with fear for Kenyatta's answer.

Slowly, Kenyatta began to chuckle, then he let back his head and laughed. Jug stared at him in surprise. His mind went back over what he had said, and he wondered what Kenyatta had found so funny. Killing a few whites wasn't no big thing for them.

"Naw man," Kenyatta said slowly, then watched the relief flood into Carol's face. "It would be useless murder, man. Sometime in the morning the people from the airplane will come walking in here, so what should we do? Wait and kill them also? Naw, Jug, it don't make sense just killin' for the sake of killin'. If these people had given us any trouble, well then, maybe we could have took them out of it, but they ain't did nothing to hurt us, and the sweet part about it is that there ain't nothing they can do to hurt us. If you take care of things like I've asked you to do."

"Okay, man, I dig where you're coming from, Ken. I'm goin' see to it that the business is taken care of," he said as he turned away and went out of the living room.

"Thanks," Carol said from her place on the couch. "You could have chosen the other way."

He glanced over at her coldly. "I chose the way I did, Carol, because it was the best thing for me to do. If it had helped us to kill all of you, then I would have given the order to have all of you killed," Kenyatta stated, watching her closely as he wondered about himself. It was no use lying. He was drawn to the white woman. He hadn't spared their lives only because of her, though.

Before he could say anything else, Betty came back into the living room. The tall attractive Black woman walked with a sway to her large, well shaped hips. She glanced over at the whites contemptuously. At the sight of Carol, her lips turned back into scorn. "I judge from what Jug just said, we're going to be gettin' away from here pretty soon," she asked as she stared coldly at the white woman's untied hands.

"Yeah," Kenyatta stated as he glanced up from his seat at her. His busy eyes didn't miss anything. He knew Betty too well. He could almost read her mind. He made up his mind not to allow his woman the chance to be with the white girl by herself. "You go back and tell the rest of them niggers that I said to get out of that motherfuckin' pool and get dressed. I plan on being away from this goddamn place in the next thirty minutes!"

Betty was taken aback and her face showed surprise. She had thought that Kenyatta would mess around long enough to slip the white woman off somewhere. But now she didn't know what was happening. She wondered if she had read the signs wrong. Never before had Kenyatta messed with a white woman, but for some reason she had sensed a bond between him and this one. Without another word, she turned on her heels and walked away, her hips swaying.

"I don't think your girlfriend likes me," Carol said in way of opening up the conversation.

Kenyatta only shrugged his wide shoulders. His mind was busy on their escape. "If we left soon, would daylight catch us out on the desert road?"

"No," she answered firmly. "It's at least four hours until daylight, and it won't take you but an hour to reach the highway." Carol got up and walked over to an old-fashioned desk that sat in the corner.

Kenyatta watched her as she opened the desk drawer and took out a pencil. She wrote something down on a piece of paper, then closed the drawer and came back to his chair. She glanced out of the corner of her eye to see if any of the whites who were tied up were watching. She leaned down over his chair, her hair fell down on his shoulders.

"Listen, Kenyatta. What I'm going to say I mean. You did me a favor out there when you killed my husband. Now, all this belongs to just me. But besides that, for some reason I like you, so. . . ." She slipped him the piece of paper. "There's an address and phone number on that page. If you ever need anything, help or money, just call that number. I'll be listening for your phone call," she added and laughed in her husky voice.

Kenyatta didn't even glance at the paper. He stuck it down in his pocket and he stared up into her eyes, wondering all along how much could she be trusted. He had never allowed himself to trust a white person before, and hesitated to do so now.

He smiled encouragingly at her. "Maybe, Miss Carol, I'll one day take you up on that. None of us really knows what tomorrow might bring. By the way, where is this address located?"

"In Los Angeles," she answered simply.

"Uh huh. I don't know what gives you the idea that I'm going there instead of to Las Vegas, but in case I should get out to sunny California, I'll make it a point to give you a ring."

Carol nodded her head and returned to her seat. She had barely sat down when Betty came in, followed by Eddie-Bee and his woman. Eddie-Bee was almost drunk, and his woman wasn't any better off.

Kenyatta glanced at them, his anger growing. "Take them drinks and dump their fuckin' heads in some water, Betty. See to it that they're ready to ride in ten more minutes!" Kenyatta stood up, his eyes blazing. "Eddie-Bee, I ain't goin' tell you but one more time, nigger. You fuck around and let that shit fuck you up when I need you again, and God will bless you, and digs will dress you, boy, and I mean every word of it!"

Before Eddie-Bee could say too many more words and get Kenyatta really riled, Betty had him and his woman back out of Kenyatta's sight. Jug came in, smiling. "Hey man, it ain't no way for these people to reach the outside now. They had a short wave set, but it won't work again no matter who the hell works on it!"

"Good!" Kenyatta stated. "Have your people get some water containers, then be ready to leave in the next eight minutes!" Kenyatta ordered sharply.

Kenyatta glanced at his watch. His small group was almost ready to leave. He sent Jug outside to get the two cars they needed to travel in. The women came out of the rear of the ranch house carrying Red between them. He was managing to walk with their help, a short snub-nosed revolver hung from his shoulder holster.

Kenyatta grinned at him. "Well, baby, looks like you goin' make it." He turned to the tall red-headed white woman. "Carol, ain't no use me re-tying you. You can cut your friends loose in a few minutes. Just don't let any of them try leaving any-time soon. The dune buggies have all been worked over, but one of them shouldn't take more than an hour to put back together, so you people won't have it too bad. As soon as daylight comes, you'll be gettin' a lot of company from the passengers from the airplane." He took one more glance at the tied whites, and turned his back and started for the door. He stooped in the doorway and glanced back at the redheaded woman. "Who knows," Kenyatta said, his parting shot, "maybe one day we'll meet again." He laughed, and with that laugh he left behind him a white woman who would spend many sleepless nights thinking about the tall Black man who had come into her life so suddenly, only to disappear after leaving his mark on her.

As Carol rushed to the window for one more look at the Black man who had so badly upset her, she heard the motors of two cars roar to life. She was in time to see the rear lights of the Cadillac and the Buick convertible leaving the ranch yard as they turned onto the dirt road that led to the highway.

8

DETECTIVE BENSON WALKED around the airport slowly, waiting on the call that would let him know that his flight was ready. His partner, Detective Ryan, had parked himself inside the bar and hadn't come out. Their evening flight had been canceled because of a flash storm. As he thought about their trip, his name was called out over the intercom. He rushed back toward the departing ramp that they were to use. Ryan met him there.

"Damn," Benson said as his partner came running up. "I'm surprised to see that you can still make it around on your own power!"

"Shit!" Ryan cursed loudly, "if you call this my own power, you're not aware of the power of the four horsemen."

Both men laughed as they walked out toward

the private airplane that was waiting to take them west. Each man carried his own suitcase and an overnight bag.

"Our big chief didn't call with any last minute advice, did he?" Ryan inquired.

"Hell, if you didn't receive any calls, Ryan, I don't know why in the fuck you should think I did," Benson stated as they neared the airplane.

Before they went aboard, three well dressed men came hurrying up. All of them seemed to be in their late twenties. One of them removed a Federal badge from his pocket and introduced the men to each other.

"My most commonly used name is Carl," he said by way of introduction, "but these other two gentlemen like it more formal. The tall one is Evans, and the blond-headed guy is Steveson. In case you forget the right pronunciation, just call him Steve."

The five law enforcement officers shook hands all around. Benson was surprised at the youth of the Federal man called Evans. He appeared to be just barely twenty-one, but from past experience, Benson knew he must be a good man or he wouldn't be assigned to this case.

After the five officers boarded the airplane, the men removed their coats and made themselves as comfortable as possible. Long holsters hung down from each man's shoulder. The Federal man who called himself Carl wore two .38 police specials hung from specially-built holsters.

The young, attractive stewardess who waited on the men was shocked at first by so much hardware. But before the airplane left the ground, she had become accustomed to the sight of the weapons. She knew that they were Federal men, so the sight of the weapons hadn't shocked her that much.

"Benson," Steveson called out, "we hear you and your partner are damn near experts on this militant organization. Is that true?"

Benson shook his head. "I don't know what you mean by experts, but we do know the people we are after a little better than most policemen."

"Good. That's damn good," Steveson stated and removed some small sketches from his briefcase. "We have some pictures here that we took at the airport. It would be of great help to us if you and your partner could put some names on a few of these damn people." Before Benson could look at the pictures, Evans spoke up. "They had a hidden camera out at the airport that took a few shots of our prey without their being aware of it. So when you finish there, maybe you could glance at these I have."

Ryan and Benson both laughed as they started to go over the pictures together. Suddenly the stewardess announced that they were about to take off, so everybody was to fasten their seatbelts. The two partners sat back beside each other and continued to go over the pictures as the jet began its takeoff. In seconds the fast-moving jet was in the air. The stewardess came around, passing out drinks. When Ryan started to reach for one, Benson stopped him.

"Goddamn it, Ben, if I needed a wet nurse I'd have asked Davidson to send one along." Even after having spoken sharply to his partner, Ryan didn't take a drink off the small tray. He had faith in his partner's judgment. Ryan knew he had a weakness for strong drink, so it came in handy having a friend around to slow him down at times.

There was not much they could do about identifying the people in the pictures. The only ones they were sure of were Kenyatta and his woman, Betty. The pictures of the other Blacks they had to pass on.

"Well," Carl said as he took the pictures into his lap and stared at them, "it was some help. At least we know what Kenyatta's woman's name is now. We had already placed that woman as being his from what people have said, and also from the way the cameras picked them up at the airport. We believe each man was walking beside his own woman, yet we can't be sure of anything. These are the most dangerous people in this country at this moment. We have been given the green light, so anything goes, just as long as we bring them in."

The other Federal men nodded their heads in agreement. All of them had the same orders. Kill the militants at the first chance, and don't take any chances.

As soon as Carl fell silent the youthful-looking Evans spoke up. "It's cases like this that I hate. I don't care what a person has done. I just despise the idea that I have an open license to kill them on sight."

"Fuck that!" Steveson said. "People like this need to be killed. Take that shoot-out at that farmhouse yesterday," he nodded at Ryan. "From what I hear, you and your partner were there, right?"

Ryan nodded his head in agreement, then took a quick glance out of the corner of his eye to see how his partner was taking it.

"Okay then, you guys were out there. Do you think it was justified the way they had to destroy those creeps? I mean, Jesus Christ, they killed seven cops! So what the hell are you going to do, play tiddlywinks with a bunch of ruthless killers like that?"

"It was one hell of a shoot-out," Ryan answered, then added, "As far as what's right or wrong, I'm in no position to answer that. I just do what I have to do."

From the tone of voice he used, the Federal man got the message—that Ryan didn't want to talk about it. The Black man sitting next to him had turned his head and was looking out the window, as if the question wasn't interesting enough for him. Steveson decided to let the matter drop as he wondered what the hell was eating these two men.

The other two Federal men had also gotten the

message. This was a subject that neither detective seemed to want to talk about.

Carl, who was the Federal man in charge of the group, thought about the matter for a few minutes, then reapproached the subject from another angle. "I don't like to bring up things that are unpleasant," he began, "but from the reactions of you two when the subject was mentioned, it seems as though you both might have some hang-ups about this that we don't know about." He fell silent, then added, "Now if it didn't have anything to do with the case, I'd just let the matter drop, but it's too important. Our very lives might depend on the way you two react to a given situation, so we might as well get the air clear on this matter."

Before Ryan could say anything, Benson spoke up. "The hang-up is not on my partner's part. It's on mine. I didn't like the idea of using tanks to blow them out, even after we had lost a few men. It was cold-blooded murder to me!" Benson said, then added, "But as far as hang-ups, we don't have any. We were responsible for the bust that went down at the farmhouse. If it hadn't been for our work, there never would have been a shoot-out, so I felt kind of bad because I knew in my heart that it wouldn't have happened if it hadn't been for me. A lot of people were wiped out at the farmhouse. Not just policemen," he stated icily.

"Yeah," was the only thing Carl could say. He ran his hands through his long, wavy black hair as his mind skipped over the trouble. Here was a Black detective, a good one true enough, but one who hated to see his people killed. He would have to give this matter a lot of thought before he made his report back, Carl reflected coldly.

Well, Ryan thought as he listened to his partner, it had been a good assignment as long as it lasted. He had no doubts about the matter. He believed the young Federal man would report back that Benson wasn't up to the job ahead, and if they took Benson off, he wanted off too.

"Well gentlemen," Ryan said quietly, "you asked my partner and he told you. Whatever he said, you can bet that I feel the same way, so whatever your thoughts are on the matter, don't just think that it's him. Put me right beside him, because whichever way he goes, I go the same way."

"So it's like that, huh?" Carl asked before anybody else could say anything. The jet hit an air pocket and the airplane did a deep dip that made all of them clutch at their seats.

"That's beautiful," Evans said. "How long have you two guys been working with each other?"

Ryan smiled, then replied, "It's been over ten years, but that's not the case either. Though Benson saved my life yesterday, that still wouldn't make any difference if I thought he was wrong. But in this case I don't. Tanks were brought in, and the people who tried to surrender were shot down. I know how he felt about it, because I felt the same way. I don't care what the person has done. Once his hands or her hands are in the air, you're supposed to take them alive."

"Well now, that puts a different slant on the thing altogether. I didn't know it had gone down like that," Carl replied. "But since you've made it very clear, I'm going to forget all about this little conversation." As soon as he finished speaking, he laid his head back and pretended as if he had fallen asleep.

The rest of the detectives started doing the same thing, while Benson continued to stare out the window.

The law enforcement officers hadn't been airborne a good two hours when the stewardess came back. "I have a radio message for Mr. Carlton Saunders."

"Right over here, miss," Carl called out. The stewardess gave Carl a folded note.

Carl quickly opened it and scanned the message. His brows seemed to come together as he concentrated on what he was reading "Gentlemen," he began, waiting to make sure he had everyone's undivided attention. "We have a slight problem on our hands. A little more information on the whereabouts of our murderers." He glanced around at all the interested faces, then continued. "It seems that Kenyatta and his gang ran into a little trouble. The airplane that they had taken control of was forced to land on the Nevada desert. From the information that I have here, the passengers have been reached. Now our problem is, whether or not it would be worth our time to stop and talk to the passengers or keep on." He held up his hand to cut off the questions, then added. "Now, we were on our way to Los Angeles, but now we might just have to change our plans. I believe we might be able to gain some kind of information from the stranded passengers, so I think it would be beneficial to our pursuit if we talked with some of them."

"It doesn't seem as if we would be going out of our way if we stopped. Hell," Evans stated, "it's not much difference from Los Angeles to any parts of Nevada, as long as we don't get lost on one of the reservations," he ended lamely and chuckled at his joke.

"What part of the desert did they land on?" Ryan asked abruptly.

"Right out of Las Vegas," Carl replied. "Now, if no one objects, I'll go up front and have the pilot land in Las Vegas instead of going on to California. After we speak to the passengers we just might come up with something that might help. Somebody on the damn plane might have overheard something that could be important to us."

"You never can tell," Steveson said as Carl got up and started toward the front of the plane. The officers began to speak amongst themselves. They wondered if this might not be the break they needed.

Benson hoped silently that it was. He thought about his wife, and hoped that this assignment wouldn't keep him away from her too long. He was getting too old to stay away months at a time. Maybe ten or fifteen years ago it might have been okay, but not now. Benson valued the quiet evenings he spent at home with his wife, or at least valued the evenings he used to spend with her until he got caught up on this damn case.

Each officer seemed to be reflecting on the Federal agent's statement. If Carl was right and they did get a break out of talking to the passengers, it would solve a lot of problems for everyone.

When Carl came back from the radio room, he wore a serious expression. He sat down and began to curse.

"Goddamn it, we have got to bring these murdering sonsofbitches to earth. They've shot up the airplane, killing, hell, I don't know how many passengers. It must have been one hell of a shootout because they lost two of their people. They want us to go straight to the place when we arrive and see if we can't help to identify the two Black militants who were killed. It seems there are some rumors running around about one of the dead Blacks being Kenyatta. I don't think we can be that lucky though. But since they don't have any prints on the man, it's up to us to let them know if they have our man."

Somehow Benson knew before ever seeing that body that it wouldn't be Kenyatta, It was just a case of all Blacks looking alike, as far as he was concerned. All Blacks looking alike was something whites were quick to assume. Yet, it seemed to Benson that Blacks were easier to tell apart than any of the long-haired honkies he came in contact with. Because of the long hair, he reasoned, most whites had something in common.

In another hour the pilot was instructing them to fasten their seat belts. The airplane had hardly touched down when two cars began to run alongside. Benson stared out at the racing cars.

"Boy, oh boy," he said, "somebody mighty damn important must be aboard this plane!" He glanced at the other members and they smiled.

"It's not that," Evans said jokingly. "They just don't want to make any mistakes and make sure you guys aren't sneaking in any of that northern fruit."

The men laughed easily amongst themselves. The strain had been broken, and now they felt as if they had something in common. They were a working team, like a small combat unit that had to depend on just itself against the enemy.

As soon as the plane stopped, the men were at the door. They didn't waste any time departing from the airplane. An elderly heavyset, red-faced man got out of the lead car and approached them. He flipped open his wallet and revealed his badge. "I'm Billings," he stated in a husky voice. "I'm supposed to show you boys around." He readjusted the large white cowboy hat he wore, then took a quick glance out of the corner of his eyes as the tall Black officer shifted one of his bags around. The man was surprised to see Benson with the group but tried not to reveal it. His orders had been to pick up some big wheel Federal men at the airport and show them around any parts of the city of Las Vegas as they thought fit to see. But he had never imagined a Black man being in the group.

"The first thing we'd like to do is see the bodies of the Blacks who were killed on the plane. After that, we'd like to question as many of the passengers as we can," Carl said.

"Well, I believe all of that can be arranged without too much difficulty. The passengers haven't arrived yet, but by the time we finish at the morgue they should have arrived."

"Oh, they haven't gotten the passengers back from the plane yet?" Evans asked.

The Las Vegas Federal man was as much surprised by the baby-faced Evans as he was by seeing the Negro in the group. He stammered but managed to ask, "I'd like to see some kind of identification from at least one of you gents." He was stuttering profusely. "It's these damn rules," Billings alibied, "you guys know what I mean." He smiled broadly, letting them know that he knew that they were all right, but he was just going by the books.

Carl, a good judge of character, knew why the man suddenly asked for proof of who they were, but didn't mind. He removed his wallet as they started for the cars and flipped it back, revealing the badge. "Don't let it worry you," Carl answered as he smiled back at the man, putting him at ease.

"We had better use both cars. There's no reason for us to be all cramped up in one car, is there?" Billings inquired.

Ryan was visibly relieved about not having to ride piled up in one car. He veered over toward the rear car, and Benson followed with Evans right on his heels. The three men got in the second car and relaxed. The white driver was another middle-aged police officer. Benson wondered idly if they had any young officers on the force. This one also wore a large, white Stetson hat.

"I'm Gary," the man said, introducing himself. He was tall and thin, with a gaunt face. His cheeks were hollow as though he didn't have any back teeth.

The three men introduced themselves, one at a time, until everybody in the car knew each other by name. Gary turned on the air conditioner in the car. "I hope this air doesn't bother any of you, but the heat out here gets so intense at times that a person has to have an air conditioner damn near everywhere he goes."

Gary fell in behind the other car that was being driven by Officer Billings. The two cars picked up speed as soon as they left the crowded airport. Soon, there was nothing but arid sand and tumbleweeds rolling along on the sandy floor of the desert.

"How long do you think it will be, Gary, before they get all the passengers off the desert?" Benson asked.

Gary glanced in the mirror to see who he was speaking with. "Oh, I don't know, boy. It shouldn't take too long because they sent three large helicopters out to pick them up," Gary stated, drawing the words out with a heavy Texas accent.

Benson had to swear under his breath, then he took the only course he thought he had. If he was going to have to work with these hillbillies, he swore he'd be damned before he'd allow them to talk to him as if he was some young ass punk they had just picked up.

"By the way, Gary," Benson began, "I don't know if you have a hearing problem or what, but I'll tell you once again, my name is Benson. That's Benson. Ben for short. Now if you should have any fuckin' trouble rememberin' it, just try calling me Mister until your mind works right."

"By God, boy," Gary began, but this time Ryan cut him off.

"The name the officer gave you was Benson, Gary. If you have any more trouble remembering it, maybe when we get back to your headquarters we'll be able to find a driver who has a better memory!" Ryan's voice was so cold that there was no doubt in anyone's mind whether or not he would follow up the threat. He would report the officer, and Gary knew that he would be taken off the big case immediately. These other officers had been shipped a long way because of this case, so their voice would be heard if and when they ever decided to say anything.

The first car pulled up in front of a modern building. As the people in the first car got out, the second one pulled up. Benson got out and waited for Ryan to reach him on the sidewalk. Again, Evans came hurrying up. Benson smiled at the younger man. Ryan and Benson could tell that Evans had taken a liking to them. He had begun to hang around them like a shadow.

Gary approached them. "Well, we might as well go in," he said. When there was no reply, he just led the way toward the front entrance. It didn't take long before they had caught up with the other members of the group. They followed an employee of the morgue down a flight of stone stairs. They made a right turn and they were standing in front of a secluded room. The attendant opened the door and led the way inside.

Lying out in the middle of the floor on different slabs were two bodies. One a Black male, the other a Black woman. Benson and Ryan stepped forward and stared down at the pair.

"Violence breeds violence," Benson said quietly, then turned to his partner. "At least they got to go out at the same time," he stated as he studied the two cold bodies in front of him. "I'd say it's Zeke and his woman. What's her name, Ryan?" he asked, bringing his partner into the picture and taking the spotlight off himself.

Ryan frowned. He knew Benson knew who the woman was and what her name was. "If I remember correct, Ben, her name was Ann. Ann Jackson, or something like that. But there's no doubt about it. That's Zeke laying there. Kenyatta will miss him. This is one of his best flunkies."

"Well, I guess that's that." Carl said quietly from beside the two detectives. "Now that we have a make on them, that's two of the bastards we won't have to worry about anymore."

"Let's not speak ill of the dead," Evans said, trying to relieve some of the tension on the Black officer.

"Who gives a fuck about the dead down here?" Billings asked coldly as the men started back toward the doorway.

"These kind of places always give me the creeps," Steveson said, really depressed because of the morgue.

As Benson followed after the rest of the men he wondered if he was overly self-conscious. He imagined that maybe at times there were situations he came in contact with only because of his color. If he hadn't been a Black man, many of the things that happened while he was working on a case wouldn't have happened. No matter how he looked at it, there was no getting around it. Even with a partner who abhorred any form of discrimination, he still found himself overly responsive to any forms of racial bigotry.

"Why the shit are you dragging your ass like a

hound dog with fleas?" Ryan said, breaking the reflective mood Benson had fallen into.

"Damn, I didn't know I was that transparent,"
Benson answered as he fell into step beside Ryan.
The two men went down the stairway that led
back onto the streets. Evans and their driver were
already inside the car waiting on the two detectives. As Benson and Ryan got in, the first car
pulled away from the curb.

"What now?" Benson asked as he settled back
in the rear seat.

"I think we are on our way to meet the unfor-
tunate passengers. By the time we get through grill-
ing them, their asses will be glad to get aboard
another damn airplane," Ryan said, before remov-
ing his pack of smokes from his pocket. "Damn,"
he cursed as he balled up the empty pack and
tossed it out the window.

"You better watch yourself, Mack. You can get a
fuckin' littering ticket for less shit than that in this
state," Benson said jokingly.

For some reason the younger detective, Evans,
had fallen into a reflective mood. He stared out of
the car window from the passenger side in the
front seat. Suddenly he broke the silence and
stated what was bothering him. "That young Black
girl back there. It was obvious," he began, "that
she had been a very pretty woman." He got his
thoughts together before continuing. "Just what
the hell has a fuckin' nut like this Kenyatta got
that can make people like her follow him?" When

nobody answered his question, he went on. "I mean, I've read her dossier and she was above average. Ann was her first name I believe, and would you believe it, the broad had three years of college under her belt."

Warming up to his subject, Evans twisted around in his seat and stared at the two men in back of him. "It just beats the shit out of me, really. Here this young, attractive girl has been to college, so she's not a ghetto child who had never seen what the other side looks like. Her people saved and planned to send their daughter through college. Then she has the bad luck to run into some creep like this fuckin' Kenyatta and blows the whole ball of wax."

It was evident from the tone of voice Evans used that the man was sincere about what he was saying. He really felt sorry for the girl back in the morgue. "I'll just never be able to understand it," he finished quietly. "This kid had everything life could offer her—looks, brains, a hell of a body on her—yet she tosses everything away to follow this fucking lunatic."

"She must not have been too fuckin' smart," Gary said.

Benson gritted his teeth. Just the sound of the hillbilly's voice got on his nerves. He knew that the best thing in the world for him would be to solve this case and get the hell back where he belonged. If Gary and Billings were any indication of what the Federal officers would be like out west, he realized that he was in for one hell of a sorry time. Savagely, he bit down on the cigarette he was smoking.

Before the men could go any further with the subject, Gary pulled into what appeared to be a closed-in parking area. Only when they were inside could you tell that it was for government men and other law enforcement agencies. Police cars, unmarked and running the mill from cheap Fords up to late model Cadillacs, were parked everywhere. Signs were everywhere also, stating that parking in certain areas was for police cars only.

After Gary found a parking spot close to the elevator, the men piled out. Carl and Steveson were waiting for their arrival. Again Billings led the way. Taking the elevator upward, the men rode in silence.

Three hours later, the four out-of-town Federal agents sat around a conference table. The men compared the information they had received from the passengers. Each man had a pad and pencil in front of him, and every now and then one of them would make a note on his pad.

"Well," Ryan said quietly, "that was the damnedest three hours of wasted time we'll have to mark down, and hope it never happens again."

"I wouldn't say that," Steveson said quickly. "I realize we didn't get anything firm to go on, but now we do have an accurate count of the people we're chasing. Before, we didn't know really how many it was. And at least we know they were out at that ranch."

"Big deal," Ryan said in disgust. The consequence of the day was wearing him down. He seemed to be drowsy or just fed-up, and it was evident in his bearing.

"Now just hold on there," Carl said lightly. "We can't afford to let little setbacks wear us down. This case isn't going to be busted overnight, so we might as well just make our minds up to the fact that it's going to be one of those cases that takes plenty damn endurance. Getting down on each other will not help a goddamn thing. So, from now on, I don't want to hear anybody knocking another officer, you guys understand?" He stared around at the three officers in his charge. "Good," he stated, then continued. "From what I could gather, either Kenyatta and his people are here in Las Vegas or they've gone on to Los Angeles."

"I'll buy that," Benson said. "I believe they pushed on toward Los Angeles. From what the people from the ranch said, I get the feeling that Kenyatta was trying to set up the impression that he was coming to Las Vegas. But from what I know of the man, Los Angeles would be more to his liking."

For the next half hour each detective offered his thoughts on the case. They had just about discussed every possible maneuver that Kenyatta and his small group could have made. Finally, Carl took his time and folded up a large map he had spread out on the round conference table.

"Now," Carl began, "as the officer in charge of this small unit I think this will be our best bet. It's not going to take all of us to stay here and check out whatever leads might come in, so we're going to split our forces. Two of us will stay here for a couple of days, while the other three go on to California. I've already made arrangements. An airplane is waiting to fly some of you guys out of here."

"That sounds great to me," Steveson said.

"I figured it would," Carl answered. "That's why I've picked you to stay here with me, Steve. He glanced over at Evans. "Now it's up to you. I'm sure that Ryan and Benson would rather go on, so I'm sending them on ahead. If you want to stay and work with us, Evans, that will be fine. If you'd rather go on with the other two men, that's fine also. It's your choice."

A large smile broke out on Evans' face. "Hey man, that's just great! Hollywood, here I come! Hell's bells, Carl, you never can tell. By the time you guys get around to arriving in Los Angeles I might have been discovered by some lucky producer. Damn man, can't you just see it now? Cop turns to acting—big hit everywhere with the broads!"

The men laughed good-naturedly, then Carl stood up. "Okay then, that's settled. Ryan, I'm putting you in charge of your group. You guys have," he took a second and glanced at his watch, "just about thirty minutes before your plane leaves. It's not a private airplane, but an unscheduled flight. This flight was set up to take as many passengers from the hijacked airplane that want to go. So you guys will see some faces you have met earlier. You just might get a tip, who knows. Maybe one of the passengers will remember something that they had forgotten, and when they see you guys just sitting there, they'll walk over and give you the big tip that will bust this case wide open."

"Oh hell yes," Evans said. "That's the only way it could go. After all, this is the west coast, and things happen out here in strange ways."

"You guys don't shit me none," Benson said, falling into the mood of trivial conversation. "You've been scheming ever since we left Michigan on how you could arrange it so that you'd have a chance to stay in Las Vegas and try and break one of the casinos."

Carl put on a convincing act of surprise. "Now I know why they call you one of Detroit's finest. Who else but a real detective could have sniffed out my intentions? Of course I'm going to bust one of the gambling tables open. This is my chance to put my foolproof system to work."

The other men laughed as they stood up. They all shook hands as they wished each other luck.

"Okay, guys," Carl said as everybody prepared

to leave. "If by chance you do get a lead on these fuckin' nuts, don't take any chances. No shit, now, we all know how dangerous our prey is, so use all the damn caution possible and then some."

"I'll give an amen to that," Ryan said as each Federal man prepared to leave. There was no telling when they would meet again, but one thing was for sure. Each agent believed in his heart that Kenyatta's days were numbered.

9
___

ON THE SOUTH SIDE of Chicago on a busy side
street, a travel-weary station wagon sat parked
and abandoned. The people who had left the car
would not have any use for it any more. Now that
they had reached their destination they wanted
nothing that might link them to Detroit, and the
Michigan license plates on the car would draw
suspicion at once.

Six blocks away, there was an old dilapidated
building that had a sign outside reading, "private
club, members only," in large red letters. The
building had once been painted a loud yellow,
but age and dirt had been to work so now it was a
dusty colored, dingy yellow. The few windows in
the front of the building had long ago given up
any pretense of being glass. Now old rotting
wood covered the window frames, even upstairs

where some sort of life seemed to exist. A Coke bottle sat on the window sill upstairs, holding up an aging window frame that was now covered with dirty plastic.

The inside of the building was the complete opposite. The floor was covered with carpet, old carpet that had seen better days, but carpet that had been kept up. The rug was of a dark brown color with dashes of red evenly spaced throughout. The furniture was similar to the carpet, old but expensive. Someone had spent money a long time ago for the few pieces sitting around. The couch and chair were French Provincial, the coloring an odd shade of gold. The coffee table was marble topped, while both end tables were matching pieces of marble. In the dining room there was an old dining set, table and chairs, with a late model china cabinet. Each of the two rooms, front room and dining room, were extra large. In the rear of the upstairs flat, the bedrooms faced each other. Besides the bathroom there were four bedrooms.

Dickie, relaxing in the chair in the front room watched the television out of the corner of his eye. His mind was not on what he was watching as he tried to listen to his host. "So you're pretty sure that was Kenyatta that took off that airplane, huh?" he asked the short, dark man sitting on the couch.

"Yeah," Tiny answered. "It ain't no doubt about

it. They flashed some of their pictures earlier, so I know what I'm talking about."

Dickie fell silent, letting the man's words sink in. It was really something to think about. If Kenyatta took the airplane, and there seemed to be no doubt about it, Dickie would have to accept it. But what really was on his mind was whether or not Kenyatta knew about the raid jumping off at the farmhouse. If he had known about that, it meant that Kenyatta had intentionally tossed the rest of his people to the dogs while he made his escape.

"I wonder," Dickie said, no longer able to hold back what was on his mind, "if Kenyatta really knew about the bust going down at the farmhouse."

"Aw man," Tiny replied quickly, "no way. You don't think our main man would be that funky, do you?"

"It's one hell of a thought," Peggy said quietly. "I mean, the way everything went down, it gives a person room to think."

Tiny wouldn't accept it. "Naw baby, it ain't no way possible for him to think like that. I mean, if he was up on it, it wouldn't have taken but a minute for him to have wired somebody up so that everybody else would know the pigs were on the way." Tiny shook his head. "Hey man, I know you and your people have had a hell of a time, but keep your mind clean. This just ain't no way to think."

Dickie wouldn't be put off that easily. "Hey, Tiny, I ain't knockin' the man, but I have to look at both sides of the coin. If I find out Kenyatta knew about the bust, he goin' have big trouble out of me."

Tiny rolled his eyes. "I mean, my man, you ain't got no reason to think like that. If you had any grounds for what you're saying, I'd dig it. But from what you've said, why do you think Kenyatta did what you think he did?"

"Why?" Dickie almost yelled. "Shit man, why in the hell did they rip off an airplane and didn't pull none of our coats that they were going? From the radio, it sounded like they were trying to take the plane out of the damn country, but just had a bad break!"

"Well, man, I don't know what to tell you," Tiny stated, then added, "but I'll bet money if Kenyatta finds out the farm was hit, he'll be calling here. This joint has been just sitting here waiting for the day it would be put into use, like now," Tiny answered sharply.

Victor entered the conversation for the first time. His woman, Irene, sat quietly beside him. "I don't know what the fuck's jumpin' off, but I'm like Dickie. I want to know why they ripped the plane off without asking any of us to go along with them."

"Maybe the man didn't know what was going to jump off until it was too late," Tiny said, still trying hard to defend Kenyatta's actions.

"Yeah, man, that ain't good enough," Dickie replied sharply. "Ain't no way I'm going to believe Ken and Zeke and the rest of them went out to the airport and instantly decided to hijack a plane. No way! It had to be planned."

"Okay, okay," Tiny said, holding his hands up. "I'm going along with that much of it. But that other shit, I can't buy it on no kind of level."

"You don't have to buy it," Victor stated coldly. "If you had been in the shoot-out at the farm, you'd be wantin' some kind of answers yourself. But as it is, you was sittin' here watchin' all that shit on television, so you don't know how hard it was!"

"Hey man," Tiny said quickly, "just wait a minute. I was cool with two main people that got killed at the farm, so I ain't takin' nothin' lightly. But on the other hand, I just can't buy that shit about Kenyatta knowing the pigs were coming. When you guys find out somethin' a person can really go along with, then pull my coat and I'll help you run down Kenyatta."

"It ain't no case of running him down," Dickie said coldly, then added, " 'cause we know damn near where we'll hold up in Los Angeles. Just like we knew to come here, we also know where the hideout is on the coast."

"I can dig it!" Tiny replied. "Everybody who's anybody knows about the hideouts, man. I know where they'll more than likely hold up at too. But it ain't got to be the real. Kenyatta plays a mean hand, Cap, so it ain't no tellin' where he might just go."

Victor leaned over and put his cigarette out in the ashtray sitting on the coffee table. "I feel like making that trip out to the coast and seeing Kenyatta myself. I don't want to take this shit up with him through the telephone. I want to look him in the eye when he's answering my questions."

"None of this shit makes sense," Tiny said. "I understand you guys' situation, so I dig where you're coming from. But man, with the attitude you guys got, I don't know what kind of transactions you might have with Kenyatta. First of all the man ain't goin' dig ya askin' him questions as if he's some kind of bitch, so you goin' have problems right there."

"Fuck the problems," Dickie said quickly. "He goin' have to stand still for our questions if we ever catch up with him."

Tiny anxiously glanced from face to face. Kenyatta was his boss and idol. The man had put him up in the pad he was staying in and sent him the rent money every month with another check just for his food at a time when Tiny didn't have a place of his own to stay. So he felt like he was indebted to Kenyatta. And even though he knew the money for the rent came out of the organization, he still felt as if Kenyatta was sending it to him personally.

With as much dignity as possible, Tiny said, "Dig, Vic, and you, Dickie. I don't mean to be out of place, man, but why don't we just wait until we hear from Kenyatta instead of sittin' here knockin' the man. You guys have made it to a hideout— one that wouldn't be here if it wasn't for Kenyatta—so let's give the man a chance."

Dickie looked at Tiny coldly. He realized at once what was on the little man's mind. At one time he also felt the same about Kenyatta as Tiny felt now. But too much had jumped off in the last twenty-four hours for him to follow Kenyatta's lead blindly. He had seen too many of his personal friends cut down from the bullets of the pigs. At first, the thought had seemed preposterous to him, but the more Dickie thought about it, the more he wondered if Kenyatta had known about the bust coming down. A year ago, it would never have entered his mind to doubt anything Kenyatta did. But now it was different. If by chance he found out that Kenyatta was guilty, justice would have to be served. No matter who was hurt, Kenyatta would have to pay for his betrayal.

At that very moment, when they sat wondering about Kenyatta, Kenyatta was entering the city limits of Los Angeles. As he drove, with Betty sitting beside him and Eddie-Bee and his woman in the rear seat, the news came over the radio. Kenyatta drove in silence as the announcer spoke of the shoot-out in the Detroit suburb. As the announcer described the gunfight on the outskirts of the city everybody listened closely, hoping and praying that some of their friends lived. When the speaker gave an estimated count of the dead, a groan went up from the listeners.

"Goddamn," Betty cursed, "it don't sound as if nobody. . . ."

Before she could finish, the announcer began to speak again, and Kenyatta waved her silent.

"There is still a heavy search going on, but now the Detroit police are wondering how a few of the participants in the gun battle escaped. They are sure that at least four or five people got away, yet they haven't given up hope of trapping the Black militants somewhere on the outskirts of the city. Roadblocks are being set up everywhere, and the fleeing gunmen are believed to be on foot. The horses the men rode when they made their wild dash for freedom have been found abandoned in the woods nearby."

"Well," Kenyatta began, "looks as if somebody made it after all," he stated. They fell silent as the realization of what he had left his people to face dawned on him. It hurt even to think about it, because he hadn't known that they would fight. He had thought that once the police pulled up, the people inside the cabins would come out and try and find out what the police wanted. A gun battle was the last thing he had thought would jump off. His well laid plans to call back and get his people out of jail were useless now. His head seemed to swell up on him as he thought about it. An exquisite pain exploded inside of him, and he knew he would never be able to get rid of the feeling of guilt whenever he thought about the farmhouse. Who got away, he wondered? Whoever it was remembered the station wagon hidden away in the woods and put the knowledge to good use. The next phase of the escape plan then would be for whoever got away to head for Chicago. If they were thinking right, Kenyatta would be able to reach the fleeing people at Tiny's.

After taking one look at Kenyatta's face, Betty turned away. She knew what her man was thinking about. She wished there was something she could do to take the look of shock off his face. Kenyatta was taking it too hard, blaming himself for everyone's death. It was silly, she reasoned, for him to think that way. It was more than that, it was preposterous. But she knew that he would fault himself. Nobody else, just he would be responsible for the people who got killed at the farm.

"Daddy," she said softly, "don't look that way. It's not your fault. Shit, who in the hell would have believed they would put up a fight? There was no reason for it. They hadn't done anything."

"If it's not my fault, then who is to blame?" Kenyatta asked sharply. "Whenever the leader lets his people down . . . , no, not let them down, neglected to inform them of what was about to jump off, there's no evasions he can use to escape the fact that he's guilty for whatever befalls them."

"Honey," she began, "you can't read the future. How the hell are you responsible for something as incredible as that gunfight? Shit it wouldn't surprise me if Ali's dumb ass didn't set it off, trying to be important."

The couple in the rear of the car were silent as they listened. Both of them knew that Kenyatta had known about the police coming, but Eddie-Bee was just finding out that Kenyatta hadn't taken the time to inform any of the people they left behind of it. Shrewdly, he remained silent. This wasn't the time to speak. It was something that he might be able to use to pull himself up in the organization at a later time. Maybe even become second in charge, next to Kenyatta.

"Whatever happened, honey," Betty stated, "it wasn't intentional. There's no reason to blame yourself for something that's out of your hands."

Kenyatta listened to her and idly wondered why it was that whenever Betty got excited her college education showed. She naturally fell into the habit of using the large words that ordinarily she wouldn't use.

As Kenyatta drove, he glanced in his mirror and wondered if Jug and those in the car behind him had heard the news over their radio. And if they had, would Jug hold him guilty for what happened back in Michigan? If there was any kind of contempt in Jug's eyes or voice when Kenyatta got around to talking to him, he wondered how he would accept it. For some reason Kenyatta valued the tall Black man behind him. Jug's opinion meant a lot.

Anxiously, Betty studied Kenyatta's face. She was

seething with worry. From past experience she knew Kenyatta was worried. He felt responsible for the people that followed him. It was as though his followers were his children, while he and Betty were the mother and father. In all probability, she reasoned, it would have happened as it did, even if he had warned them. There hadn't been enough cars there for everybody to get away. The confusion would have been enormous.

"Ken, honey," Betty said softly, "isn't there anyway you can call and find out what you want to know?" Her voice was soft and gentle.

"That's just what I was thinkin' 'bout," Kenyatta answered, as he searched the streets for a telephone. He could wait until they reached the hideout, he reasoned, but he wanted to know who escaped the massacre before then. They had at least another half an hour of driving before he'd reach the place in Watts. Suddenly he noticed a pay telephone sitting next to an open lot. He hit his car blinker, letting Jug know that he was turning, then made a sharp turn up onto the lot. Before he got out of the car, Jug had pulled in behind him.

Kenyatta fished in his pockets for a dime and, when he couldn't find one, he glanced over at Betty. She was holding the coin he needed in the tips of her fingers. It was at times like this that he wondered about her. Did she read his mind? It seemed at times as if she knew his thoughts as well as he did.

Jug climbed out of .his car and approached Kenyatta. As he came up, he called out. "I guess you heard the news too, huh?"

Kenyatta just shook his head as he stared at the tall man, trying to figure out how the news had affected Jug.

"It was a sad affair," Kenyatta answered, still staring closely at Jug. No matter how hard he concentrated, he couldn't determine whether or not Jug was angry. Kenyatta's thinking was influenced quite a bit by the guilt he felt already, so it was easy for him to believe everybody else thought him wrong.

"I know, man," Kenyatta stated, "you think it was my fault our people back there got wasted, don't you?"

"I don't think a goddamn thing, man," Jug answered harshly, then added, "What happened happened. We got enough problems on our hands already without me worrying about some other shit. Red done went into another bag, man. He's full of fever or something. He's raving out of his head. While we were on the highway it was all right, but in the city we're going to be in trouble if he keeps screaming the way he does."

As though to prove his point, a loud scream came from the parked car behind them. Kenyatta glanced nervously back at the car. "Damn!" he exclaimed. "I see what you mean. Well, Jug, we ain't goin' be here but a minute, so hold on. I want to make a call back east and see who got clear of that shit. After that, we'll head for Watts. If we're lucky, we'll make it without any troubles."

Jug glanced back at the car he was driving, then removed a pack of cigarettes from his pocket. "Let me get a light from you," he said, as the smoke dangled from his mouth.

Kenyatta gave him a book of matches, then walked over to the telephone. In seconds he had placed the call and Tiny's voice came over the receiver. "Hey man," he said, "what's happenin' back there?"

For a second Tiny was too dumbfounded to answer. Then, "Hey, my man, is it really you?" Tiny asked, shocked.

"Who the hell do you think it is? Your daddy?" Kenyatta joked as he smiled at the man's surprise.

"Dig this, man," Tiny began. "Dickie and Victor and their ladies are here man, so what's the deal? You want me to put them on the phone?" Tiny asked, waiting patiently for an answer.

Kenyatta hesitated briefly. He didn't want to get caught up in a long telephone call. Then just as quickly he checked himself, calling himself a coward. You're only trying to evade the truth, he thought coldly, You don't want to speak to any of them niggers 'cause you're afraid one of them will call you out over that shit that jumped off.

Kenyatta stood there arguing it out with himself until Tiny's voice came over to him.

"Hey, Kenyatta, what you want me to do, man? Put one of them on the telephone? Can you hear me all right?"

"Yeah, man, yeah," Kenyatta replied. "Go ahead, Tiny, put Dickie on. I might as well take a second to get this shit straightened out," Kenyatta said, speaking more to himself than to the man on the other end of the telephone.

"Okay, brother," Tiny answered, then walked away from the phone, shaking his head. "Hey, Dickie, somebody wants to rap to you on the bitch box."

Dickie jumped up and rushed to the telephone. "Hey man," he yelled over the line, "what's the deal?"

"Dig, Dickie," Kenyatta said quickly. "I can't take but a second, man. Red's been shot, and he's out of his head, so I got to get him off the streets. I just heard over the news about the shoot-out. Goddamn man, I couldn't believe my ears."

"You couldn't, huh," Dickie answered, unable to figure out a way to ask the questions he wanted so desperately to ask.

"Yeah man, it came as a complete shock to me," Kenyatta stated, not wanting to give the man a chance to get off into something that would be embarrassing to him. He could sense the man's desire to ask him something, but he wanted to avoid that moment as long as possible.

"Dig, Dickie," Kenyatta said quickly, "like I said, we're on the run, man. We're ridin' in two hot cars and we got a long way to go before we reach a safe place, so I can't waste any more time talkin' right now. But as soon as I've got my people safely hid, I'll call back and let you and your group know where we're at. Maybe we can all get together out here. I don't know right now, but after I've had time to think about it, I'll wire you up on it."

"Okay, man, but dig this. Why . . . ?" Before Dickie could ask the question he had made up his mind to ask, the telephone went dead. He stood holding the receiver in his hand, staring at it dumbfounded.

"What's the matter, honey?" Peggy asked as she came into the dining room where the telephone was. "You act like you just ran into a ghost or something."

Dickie slammed the telephone down. "Shit!" he cursed loudly. "Motherfucker!" He realized that his chance to get the questions that were bugging him settled was gone. He had let it slip through his fingers. Kenyatta hadn't wasted any time hanging up. But if he was trying to be honest, he could understand the man's haste.

Victor came into the room. "Did you find out why or what he knew about the bust?"

"Naw, man," Dickie replied, still warm with himself. "I didn't have the time."

"Didn't have the time!" Victor repeated sharply. "Well I'll be damn!"

"Yeah, man, you just be that," Dickie said

coldly. "The man was in a hurry, Vic. When I went to ask him, he hung the telephone up."

"He probably heard you, man, but didn't want to reply," Victor said loudly.

Tiny walked back into the dining room and listened to the conversation closely.

"Naw, Vic, it wasn't like that, man. He was tellin' me 'bout Red being shot and ravin' out of his head. Then some more shit about they were a long ways away from the hideout and ridin' in two hot cars, so he didn't want to waste any time."

"Didn't want to waste any time," Victor said sarcastically. "Shit, man, he just didn't want to talk, that's all!"

"Hey man, you guys just don't want to give my man no kind of break, do you?" Tiny asked sharply, his temper rising.

Dickie whirled around on Tiny. "Say, my man, why don't you get off our back, huh? We got enough troubles without you jumpin' in our conversations without anybody askin' you!"

Tiny bristled at the tone of Dickie's voice. "Dig this, chump! Didn't nobody ask ya here, man, and ain't no damn body holdin' no gun on you makin' you stay! So if you don't like the way I carry myself, you know what you can do. The doors always open both ways!"

"Shit," Victor swore harshly. "This joint belongs to us just as much as it does you, Tiny, so if anybody leaves, it ain't goin' be us until we're damn ready!"

Seeing the formidable look on both the men's faces, Tiny began to back down. "I ain't meanin' nothin' funny, man, but the way you guys keep knockin' Kenyatta, I just can't dig your stayin' at his place if you ain't got no faith in the man."

"His place," Peggy said scornfully. "Shit, Tiny, we all paid dues to keep these joints open, so ain't nothing just Kenyatta's. Everything belongs to everybody in the goddamn organization—whatever's left of it, anyway," she finished harshly.

"So just be cool man, okay?" Dickie said, trying to change the subject. He didn't want to argue with the short man. They all had to live together, so the last thing they needed was misunderstandings between them.

"We don't mean to be knockin' the man, Tiny," Dickie added. "We're just going over what went down. I can see the reason why he hung up so fast myself. He's got a hurt man on his hands, plus the cars they're driving are hot as hell, so he's moving fast. He said he'd get back to us as soon as possible, Vic, and he'd be thinkin' 'bout ways of gettin' us together, so it might not be as bad as you think. The man's under a hell of a lot of pressure, so let's give him a chance to straighten this shit out. We ain't in no kind of hurry."

Victor shook his head in agreement, but he didn't like it worth a damn. He felt as if Kenyatta could have taken the time to explain something to them. The man seemed to be evading something, as far as he could see, and he wondered just why Kenyatta would be doing it. It wasn't like him to evade an issue, so something must be on the man's mind. Maybe, Victor reasoned, it was like the man said. He had a wounded man on his hands and was worried because they were riding in stolen cars. As he made his way back to his seat, he decided he'd play a waiting game. Time was on their side, so all they had to do was to wait. Kenyatta would have to come out with the truth sooner or later. And better sooner than later!

10

THE RIDE ON THE airplane was quiet and un-
eventful. When the plane landed, Ryan and
Benson got off first, followed by Evans. The three
men made their way through the airport quickly,
then waved down a cab at the front near the parking lot. It was a warm day and the three policemen removed their coats once they were inside
the cab.

"Well," Ryan began, "we finally arrived." The
statement fell on deaf ears. The other two men
didn't bother to comment.

The white cab driver glanced in his mirror at
the hardware his passengers were wearing. The
sight of the open display of guns frightened the
man, but after they gave their destination, the driver
relaxed. He wondered idly why the officers hadn't
had a police car pick them up instead of paying

out all the money it would cost them to reach police headquarters.

Their first stop was the police department of the City of Los Angeles. Here they were assigned a uniformed driver who knew his way around the city.

"Since you're in charge," Benson said, egging his partner on, "what do we do now? I'm kind of tired of standing around with my finger up my ass trying to look important for these other assholes who keep watching us."

"Hey man, that's right," Evans said as he smiled broadly.

"Fuck both of you," Ryan replied, then added, "Why don't we get the hell out of here anyway? Give our driver a chance to get used to the car and all that shit."

"Good enough with me," Benson answered. "Where the hell are we going though?"

"Hell, I don't give a shit if we don't go anywhere but to the nearest restaurant. We haven't had a decent meal since leaving Detroit." Ryan beckoned at the tall, heavyset policeman who had been assigned to their case.

"Hey, buddy," Ryan called out, "you want to bring the car around to the front, or should we all just go downstairs with you and get in it there?"

"It's all the same with me," the officer replied as he shrugged his wide shoulders.

"Good enough," Ryan answered. "Why don't you just lead the way then?"

The three men followed the uniformed officer into the elevator. The ride downstairs to the underground garage was silent as each man kept his peace. After reaching the unmarked car, the three men piled in, with Ryan getting in the front seat next to the driver.

"Hey, boss man," Benson called out, "who the hell is going to pay for the food? Not me, I hope."

"I don't know why in the hell not," Ryan replied quickly. "Since you're not doing a damn thing to earn your money, you might as well share it with us."

"Like hell I will," Benson answered.

The driver glanced in his mirror as he wondered about the three men he was ordered to drive around. There was no doubt in his mind about their importance. It wasn't every day that three officers came from out of state. Whatever case they were on had to be an important one. Maybe, he hoped, if he played his cards right, he might come out of this thing with a promotion.

When the men arrived at the restaurant that Evans had directed them to, Ryan invited the driver inside with them for lunch. But the man declined, saying he would stay and listen for any police calls that might be of interest to them.

After a quick briefing, Ryan got out of the car. The three men entered the restaurant together. They took their time ordering, since they didn't have anything else to do. When their meals came, they sat and toyed with their food like little children.

"You know," Benson began, "I feel like a complete ass. Here we are, out-of-town policemen, while they got a damn good police force right here. They need our help about as much as a dog needs fleas."

"It's not as bad as all that," Evans said quietly. "I know how you feel though. Here we don't have a fuckin' thing to do, but once we go over to the Federal Building, we're going to have to spend some time briefing a lot of officers on whatever we know about the suspects."

"And that's damn little," Ryan stated loudly. "We don't really know a fuckin' thing more than any other policeman who has read up on this case."

"That may be true," Evans admitted, "but the big wigs don't look at it that way."

The three men laughed, then argued over who would pick up the check. It didn't matter though. They were all carrying expense money. Evans was finally ordered by the other two to pay for the meal, since Federal men made more money than regular policemen.

When they returned to the police car, Evans asked the driver to take them over to the Federal Building. The drive was short, and before they had time to light a cigarette, they had arrived.

As soon as they parked, the radio began to hum. The driver turned up the volume so that everybody in the car could hear the call.

"A gunfight involving a Buick convertible with license number LIC 9294 is underway. A Cadillac with unidentified license number was believed to be in the gunfight also," the voice over the box said.

"Goddamn," Evans managed to say. "I believe that's our people." He was yelling loudly.

"Driver," Ryan snapped out, "get us over to the scene of that fuckin' gunfight as quick as this buggy will move!" He turned in the seat and grinned at his two partners. Evans was busy checking the license number he had just heard against the numbers he had written down inside his notebook. "Yeah," Evans said excitedly, "those are our boys all right! There's no dull moments when Kenyatta's around."

"I just hope they pin those bastards down," Benson prayed as the car leaped away from the curb.

"What about the siren?" the driver asked. "Is it all right if I turn it on?"

"Goddamn right," Ryan said, his voice pitched to a high note of excitement.

"What do you think went down?" Benson asked as all three of the men waited impatiently to arrive at the scene of the shoot-out.

"Probably some patrol car picked up the hot license numbers. They went out immediately to all law enforcement agencies," Evans answered, his eyes bright with the rising tension.

The driver pulled out all stops. He pushed the

gas pedal to the floor and raced dangerously through the slow moving traffic. As soon as he

cleared the downtown area, he pulled up on the freeway and continued to drive as though all their lives were in danger. The cars on the freeway pulled over to the right and let the speeding, wailing car through.

"About how long will it be before we get there?" Ryan asked the driver.

The driver hesitated, then replied, "We should be gettin' there in another five minutes."

"Good," Ryan answered, then removed his gun and started checking the loads. The other two officers began to do the same thing.

As they rode, Benson prayed silently for the Lord to make it possible for them to end their chase today. If only Kenyatta would be driven into a dead-end street or something. Anything that he couldn't get out of. Any other damn crook would have been captured by now. But Kenyatta seemed to live a charmed life.

"I'll bet that bastard gets away before we even get there," Benson said gloomily.

Ryan glanced back at him. "With your fuckin' outlook, our long shot hasn't a chance of payin' off."

"It might not be such a long shot after all," Evans stated. "If a couple of patrol cars are on their ass, they don't have any chance of getting away."

Suddenly their radio exploded with noise, then an officer's voice was heard, pleading. "Help! This is a code alert. Two officers are down with gun-shot wounds. We need help immediately!" The sounds of gunshots were clearly heard over the radio. It was as though somebody had leaned down into the police car where the call was coming from and opened fire.

"Goddamn, goddamn, the police-killing sons-ofbitches!" Ryan's voice was all choked up as he cursed.

"Step on it, driver," Evans called out sharply from the backseat, "we ain't got all day!"

The remark irritated the driver but he didn't reply. He just pushed his foot down harder on the gas pedal. The traffic cleared up in front of them, and he neatly went in and out of two cars that were slowing down to let him past.

"I got a feelin' we goin' be too late," Benson said again, but this time there were no comments.

11

——

AFTER MAKING THE telephone call, Kenyatta walked slowly back to the car Jug was in. The morning traffic was beginning to get lighter as most of the early morning workers had already made their way to work.

"Jug, we ain't got that much farther to go. You want to let Eddie-Bee drive, while you take a break and ride with me?"

Without hesitation Jug agreed. He was tired of listening to Red's screams, so anything would be better than having to put up with the wounded man. "Yeah, Ken, it might just give my nerves the break they need," he said as both men started back toward the Cadillac.

Kenyatta leaned down toward the rear window. "Eddie, how about you relievin' Jug? He's tired after driving on the highway all night. I might just let Betty take over in this one."

Eddie-Bee climbed out of the car, with his woman Jeannie right behind him. The short, dark-complexioned woman looked like a man as she got out. The pants suit she wore didn't help any. Jeannie was husky, and when she spoke her voice was as heavy as a man's.

"How damn much farther have we got to ride?" she asked Kenyatta as she climbed out.

"Not much farther," he replied, watching the street traffic for any signs of danger.

"Good," Jeannie said as she tried to rub some of the sleep out of her eyes. Her short natural was messed up, while her eyes had become bloodshot from lack of proper rest.

"You goin' need some gas in that piece," Jug told Eddie-Bee as the man started toward the car in the back of them. Eddie-Bee stopped and waited to hear what Kenyatta had to say.

"I need refueling myself, so just follow me into whatever gas station I pick out," Kenyatta said.

There was a loud scream that made all three of the men jump. Its sound was eerie in the morning air. "Damn, that scared the shit out of me," Eddie-Bee said truthfully.

"It's only Red," Jug stated calmly. "He's been doing that shit for the past hour or so."

Even as Jug spoke, the car door opened and his woman, Almeta, climbed out. She looked exhausted. "Damn," she cursed as she came abreast of the men, "Red seems to be gettin' worse."

"Well there ain't a damn thing we can do for him here," Kenyatta stated honestly. "If we push on, maybe in an hour or so we'll be somewheres where we can get some help for him. But as long as we're on the road ain't nothing we can do but pray our luck holds out."

"Yeah, man," Jug said as Eddie-Bee started to walk back toward the car he was supposed to drive. "I been wonderin' for the past hour if they got these license numbers yet?"

Kenyatta shook his head. "It's hard to guess on that, Jug. I know by now they should have reached the people stranded out at the ranch, so it's likely that they do have the number. It must have took us four good hours or more to make this drive, so we can't do nothing but hope for the best, while keepin' our guns at the ready."

"I'll buy that, my man. If it goes down, I'd rather hold court out here in the streets than let them motherfuckers get me down to one of them stations and throw the fuckin' book at me! Shit," Jug continued, "it ain't no kind of doubt in my mind what kind of time we goin' get. They might even bring back the death penalty for our ass!"

"You can bet your ass on it, Jug," Kenyatta replied. "These white motherfuckers would love nothing better than to see us sittin' in the hot chair!"

As Kenyatta spoke, he reached out and opened the car door on the driver's side. "I guess we had best be gettin' on." Jug started around the car with his woman following him.

They didn't speak any more until after they got in the car, then it was Almeta who broke the silence.

"Shit," she began, "I wish we could make it to the damn hideout without stoppin' for gas. The way Red's actin' up back there, it's goin' be touch and go if we have to pull into a damn gas station."

"Maybe we can find a gas station with a Black attendant working," Kenyatta said. "That way we stand a better chance. Niggers aren't as suspicious as whites. If a honkie sees Red stretched out on the car seat yelling his head off, he's goin' call the police station the first chance he gets!"

"I don't know why you think a brother is going to be any different," Jug said. "Shit, nowadays, the niggers are just as bad as the peckerwoods. They see a chance to get their Black faces smeared across one of the daily newspapers, and goddamn, you had better watch out! The Black motherfucker would bust his own mother for the fuckin' chance!"

Betty laughed harshly. "It ain't got that bad yet, Jug. Damn, man, give our people a little break," she said jokingly.

"I'll give them a break all right. I'll break their motherfuckin' necks if one of them gets in my goddamn way," Jug answered seriously.

Ever since he had been busted five years ago by his rap partners who had been Black, Jug had been down on his own people. He didn't give them a chance. He believed they were as bad as the whites, and in many cases he was right. At that very moment his mind slipped back into the past. He sat remembering the stickup where he got away from the robbery, while the two men he was with got busted. Before he could get back to the motel to pick up a few pieces of clothes, the police were pulling up in the parking lot. When he came out of his motel room, they had the place surrounded. A huge spotlight pinned him in the doorway as soon as he opened the door to come out. With a quick backward movement, he leaped back inside, but there had been no escape. Within seconds, the windows were shot out, and on the next opportunity they gave him to surrender, he tossed his guns out. He had never forgotten the two men who busted him, even though he had never had a chance to pay them back.

Kenyatta glanced out the window at an open gas station. Both of the attendants were white, so he kept going. Betty glanced over at the gas gauge, then stared up at her man.

"Ain't you gettin' ready to play it kind of close, honey?" she asked, then added, "If we run out of gas and have to walk and find a station open, we're going to be in big trouble, aren't we?" She waited patiently for his reply.

Kenyatta kept his eyes on the road in front of

him. Her words had rung a bell inside his head. "What if we parked near a gas station and walked back for a can of gas, Jug? You think that might work?"

Jug hesitated before answering, giving the question slow deliberation, which was his way. "I don't know, man," he said at last. "We would have to make a hell of a lot of trips with a can to fill up both cars with enough gas to make it to where we have to go, wouldn't we?"

"Not really," Kenyatta replied. "We ain't got to go but to Watts. But from here, I don't know if one can of gas would be enough for both cars."

"It seems like that would draw suspicion on us," Betty said quietly. "Hell, you'd have to park near the gas station, and when you came back for the second or third can of gas, the station attendant would have to start wondering why in the hell you didn't drive up and get the rest of it, wouldn't he?" She ended by asking a question again, always making Kenyatta think that he was really solving the problem, while she sometimes led him right up to the answer.

"Fuck it!" he exclaimed, "I'm tired of this cat and mouse shit anyway. Whatever is going to jump off is going to go down no matter what the fuck we do, so I'm going to pull into the next station I see open. No matter if the sonofabitch workin' there is a green man!" Kenyatta thus ended all discussion on the problem.

Betty sat back in the seat and let out a sigh. It

was out of their hands now. Like Kenyatta said, whatever happened would happen. She fingered the large .44 magnum inside her purse. The gun was heavy, but she liked the way it hit. Once she hit a man, she didn't have to worry about him getting back up too soon.

"There's one coming up on your right," Jug called out from the rear seat.

Kenyatta had seen the gas station himself, even before Jug spoke, but there was no sense in mentioning the fact. He just drove up into the station silently, not saying a word. He watched the gas station attendant come out. The man was white.

"Tell him to put three dollars worth in it," he told Betty. She could roll down her window and give the man the order without him having to come all the way around the car to Kenyatta's window. Betty did as she was told and watched the man as he made his way toward the pumps.

As Kenyatta watched the man filling up the tank in the mirror, he saw another attendant walk over to the car Eddie-Bee was driving. In a matter of minutes, he told himself, we'll be away from here. Everything looks as if it might go off just right.

Eddie-Bee had gotten out of the car and was standing in such a way to make it impossible for the man waiting on his car to see who was in the rear.

Kenyatta let out a sigh of relief as he saw the man putting the gas into their car start to hang up the hose. The man started toward the front of the car.

As Kenyatta began to roll his window down, he noticed a police car swing into the gas station. The officer driving the car drove straight over to the pop machine near the front door of the station. One of the policemen got out and started for the machine. It was at this instant that a shrill scream came from the car behind them. Kenyatta could hear it clearly, even though it was muffled as if someone had tried to stuff something into the screaming man's mouth.

The policeman stopped in his tracks. His eyes began to search the area for the sound. Even as he stared around dumbly, the car door behind Kenyatta opened and Red jumped out. In his right hand was a gun. He stared feverishly around. His bloodshot eyes picked up the blue uniform as the policeman stared at the wounded man in total surprise.

Before the officer could react, his partner screamed out a warning. "Watch him, Ed, he's got a gun in his hand!" The other policeman came bolting out of the driver's side of the car.

Seeing the policeman was enough for Red. He raised the pistol in his hand and fired, but his aim was off. His first bullet missed the shocked policeman by a mile. Before he could get off another shot, the second policeman cut him down. The sounds of gunfire hadn't died down when a loud boom rang out. Red's woman had let down the back window and cut the officer down who had shot her man.

The fight was on. The first officer jumped for the rear of the car. Eddie-Bee's woman had already taken aim, and before he could reach the safety he sought, two slugs from the .38 special she carried cut him in half.

Kenyatta was the first one to notice the third policeman inside the car. The man was busy on the radio. "Goddamn it," Kenyatta roared, "there's another one of the motherfuckers in the police car!"

Betty took aim after letting her window down. The shot from her gun took the policeman in the side of the head. The gas station attendant standing beside their car could only stare in shock at what was going on.

Kenyatta kicked the motor over on the large, expensive car and the Caddie came alive with a roar. "Let's get the hell out of here!" he yelled at Eddie-Bee, who had run around the car and was kneeling down beside the dying Red. At the sound of Kenyatta's voice, Eddie-Bee jumped back to his feet. Before he could regain the driver's seat, another police car came roaring up into the gas station.

"Motherfucker!" Kenyatta cursed. "The bastards are like roaches. You kill one and a hundred more come to his funeral!"

The police car pulled to the side, blocking the entrance from that direction so that nobody could get past unless they turned around.

Eddie-Bee, trapped on the outside of his car, wheeled around with his pistol in his hand. He took a quick shot at the policemen as he tried to snatch the car door open.

As Kenyatta drove slowly away from the pumps, the policemen concentrated their gunfire on the second car, believing the first one wasn't involved in the shoot-out. The call they had heard mentioned only a Buick convertible, so they had no reason to suspect the second car of any wrongdoing. Kenyatta maneuvered their car into an excellent position to cut down the unsuspecting officers. When one of the gas station attendants attempted to warn the policemen of their danger, gunfire from the Cadillac cut him down.

The sounds of the gunfire warned the policemen, but it told them about the danger too late. A barrage of bullets cut the officers down in their tracks, but not before they were able to knock Eddie-Bee off his feet.

One of the policemen staggered around from the impact of the gunshots and the gun in his hands went off. The wild bullet struck the pump. Instantly everything nearby went up in flame. The white attendant working on the car was completely covered with flames.

Screams erupted from the passengers of the

car. The two women trapped inside the burning inferno screamed at the top of their lungs.

Even as Kenyatta and his party sat watching, the car door burst open and one of the women came running out. She was covered with fire so completely that no one in Kenyatta's car could recognize who she was. Her loud screams continued while she rolled over and over.

"Motherfucker!" Jug said in shock from the backseat. "Man," he continued, "I ain't never seen nothing like this before in my life!"

The flame continued to spread as if it had a life of its own. Betty spoke up suddenly. "If we don't get out of here, we're going to get trapped in the same fire!" Her voice was shrill.

Even as she spoke, flames began to leap out of the pumps toward them. "Goddamn," Jug screamed from the back. His voice had gone up a notch in his panic. "If we don't move, man, that fuckin' pump is going to go up in a second and we'll go up with it!"

Even as Kenyatta stared out of the window dumbfounded, flames surrounded the police car, and in seconds it was a ball of fire.

"We goin' have to go through it to get out, man," Kenyatta said as he searched for the safest route out of the flaming death.

"Go on through the motherfucker then," Jug ordered harshly from the back. "We don't stand a chance if we keep sitting here!"

"We don't stand a chance if I drive straight through that wall of flame, either," Kenyatta yelled

back. Suddenly he spotted a small chance for them. The garage door was open, and it led toward the rear of the garage, which was wide open. So far the flames hadn't moved over and consumed the building.

With a vicious twist of the wheel, Kenyatta swung the car around in a quick turn and drove straight toward the door. Even as the big car picked up speed, a line of fire was leaping toward their only means of escape.

"Oh sweet motherfucker!" Betty prayed. "Don't let it end like this. Please, Lord!"

Kenyatta gritted his teeth and stomped down on the gas pedal. From the angle he had been at, he could only see that both doors of the garage were open. He didn't know if any of the racks were up or in the way. If so, there was going to be one hell of a wreck. He made the sharp turn and the big car started through the open doors. With a sigh of relief he noticed at once that nothing seemed to be in their way. In seconds they were through and rushing up the small alley. Just in time too. From behind them came the sound of a huge explosion. Jug glanced back out of the car window and cried wildly.

"Good goddamn, man! If we hadn't gotten out when we did, we'd be fried littl' niggers right this minute! That motherfucker blew sky high!"

From the mirrors on the car, Kenyatta could see what kind of death they had just escaped. "Well, we barely made it. Looks like Lady Luck is still smiling down on some of us."

"You can say that again," Betty said. "Even to the point that you saved three dollars. That poor ass attendant never did collect his money!"

The rest of the people in the car laughed, letting out the tension that had gripped them so hard. Almeta spoke up for the first time. "I still can't believe we made it," she said honestly.

"Why don't you try pinching yourself to find out if you're still with the living, then," Jug said to her with a laugh.

"Honey," she answered, "I'm so damn glad we switched cars, I don't know what to do. If we hadn't, that could have been us back there, instead of Eddie-Bee and his woman, you know?"

"I know, honey," Jug replied. "But I guess it just wasn't our time. Jug leaned over and took his woman into his arms.

"Hey," Betty said jokingly, "we can't have none of that kind of shit going on. Not until all of us can indulge, anyway," she stated with a laugh.

"Thank you, Lord," Kenyatta said under his breath, as he came to the end of the alley and started to pull out.

An unmarked police car went rushing past. The sound of the siren screaming loudly in the morning wind flooded the air.

The three plainclothesmen inside the car stared intently out the window. One of the policemen in the backseat jerked his finger at the car coming out of the alley.

"Hey!" Evans said, "there's a late model Cadillac coming out of that alley back there! He glanced back out the car window in time to see the car disappearing as it turned toward the freeway.

"What the hell do you want us to do about it?" Ryan asked. "Stop every Cadillac we see?" He hesitated, then added, "This call is too important for us to stop now, Evans. If it's there when we come back, we can check on it then."

"You don't have to worry about it being there," Evans replied. "I just saw it turn off onto the freeway."

A little later on in the day, Ryan would remember this conversation. But at the moment, his mind was too busy on what was ahead of them. "Goddamn," he cursed from the front seat, "it looks like the whole damn city is on fire in front of us, don't it?"

The other men in the car strained their eyes to see in seconds the full picture of the horrible inferno. The driver drove as close to the fire as possible, then parked and let the plainclothes officers out. The men approached on foot.

Other policemen had arrived before them. The detectives flashed their badges.

Twenty minutes later, the three detectives began

to question witnesses. It wasn't until they talked to their third witness that they heard about the Cadillac that had barely escaped the fire. The witness told them about the way the huge car had gone through the building right before the explosion.

Benson cursed. He remembered instantly the car coming out of the alley as they rushed past. He didn't mention it to his partner, though. Ryan had enough on his mind already without any guilt feelings being added. He glanced at Evans. The younger detective only shook his head.

"It goes like that at times," Benson said to Evans. Ryan overheard the remark and turned on the two men. There was a look of pain in his eyes. "I'm not a fool," he said at once, "so I'm not trying to fool myself. There was a damn good chance that the car Evans saw held Kenyatta, or whichever members of his gang were left. It could be that Kenyatta went up in that flame too."

Benson only nodded. "Yeah man, there's that chance." But deep down he knew that their luck wouldn't be that good. A man like Kenyatta wouldn't die that easily. No, they wouldn't get off the hook like that. It would take some more bloodshed like tonight before Kenyatta was brought to his knees. In the meantime, the only thing they could do would be to continue tracking down their dangerous foe. One day, though, Benson believed, they would come face to face with their sworn enemy. And when that happened, he only hoped his finger would be near the trigger of his

gun.

In all his life Benson had never really hated any of the men he had brought in. But this time, for reasons that he couldn't even understand, he hated the man he chased with a passion.

12

ON THE CALIFORNIA freeway, Kenyatta drove the big car at a reasonable speed. He didn't want to attract any undue suspicion. He was silent as he let his thoughts wander. When he had left Detroit, he had ten people with him. Now he had four. They bad cut him down to size, but he wouldn't let that get him down. What he hated was that he had lost a lot of well trained people. People who had the nerve it took to continue their private war on dope pushers and nigger-killing policemen. No matter, he reasoned. In time he would train some more dedicated Black men, and then he would continue, because there were no doubts in his mind about their cause. As long as men put on uniforms and took out their racial dislike on poor people he would continue his war on them. There was no reason to wait for the courts to cut them loose after they had killed some fourteen-year-old Black kid. No, it didn't have to go that far, not if he could help it.

"Honey," Betty said from her side of the car, "aren't we damn near there?" She spoke in that husky voice of hers.

He glanced out of the corner of his eyes at the intelligent Black woman who would follow him through hell if he asked her to. Yes, he reasoned, as long as people like her believed in him, he would continue. He noticed the ramp ahead of him. It was the one leading to Watts. In a matter of minutes he was pulling up in front of an old house. He parked the car and got out in the sunlight. He felt the strong rays of the sun on his black skin and it felt good. He was still alive, and he still had people who believed in him. It wouldn't be long before he was back on his feet. Betty came around the car and he took her arm.

Jug fell in step behind him, carrying an overnight bag. They walked away from the Cadillac and toward the main drag. All the faces they passed were Black, and that made him feel good. This was prime territory for recruiting, so it wouldn't take long at all. No indeed. With the money they had in the bag Betty carried, it wouldn't take long at all. Before he was finished, Los Angeles would know that he had arrived. And he'd bet his last dollar on that—against a bucket of shit!

"Honey," Betty said, "what we gonna do when we get there?"

Kenyatta was silent for a minute, concentrating on the road ahead of the speeding car. Then he glanced over at his woman and smiled.

"Same thing we've always done, honey," he replied. "Only our job's just a little bit harder this time. We got to get this organization set up all over again."

"Then we got to get more people. Right?"

"Right. And we'll get them easy enough. There's lots of Blacks who feel the same way as we do, and they'll make good organization people. It won't be long, and then we'll be in business again!"

The car speeded toward Watts.

Don't miss any of the books in the
Kenyatta series.

Here's a peek at Donald Goines's

Crime Partners and *Death List*

Available now from Holloway House Classics!

From *Crime Partners*

1
___

Joe Green, better known to his friends and acquaintances as "Jo-Jo," poured the rest of the heroin out of a small piece of tinfoil into the Wild Irish Rose wine bottle top that had been converted into what drug users call a "cooker."

His common-law wife, Tina, watched him closely. "Damn, Jo-Jo, I sure hate the thought of that being the last dope in the house. The last time your slow-ass connect said he would be here in an hour, it was the next day before the motherfucker showed up!"

Shrugging his thin shoulders philosophically, Jo-Jo didn't even glance up at his woman as he replied. "That's one of the few bad points you run into when your connection doesn't use. They don't understand that a drug addict has to have that shit at certain times. It ain't like a drunk; when Joe

Chink says it's time to fix, it's time to fix, with no shit about it."

"Jo-Jo, you don't think the bastard will do us like he did last time, do you?" she asked, her voice changing to a whining, pleading note.

"Goddamn it," Jo-Jo yelled as he patted his pockets, "I ain't got no motherfuckin' matches." He glanced around wildly, his eyes searching in vain for a book of matches on one of the trash-covered end tables.

The house they lived in was a four-room flat. You could enter by either door and stare all the way through the house. The back door led right into the kitchen, which went straight into the dining room, or bedroom, whichever you wanted to call it. The bed came out of the wall, Murphy bed style, and could be put up into the wall after use but never was in this particular house. After the dining room came the front room. Here there had been some sort of effort to gain a partial amount of privacy with a long, filthy bedspread that had been tacked up and stretched across the rooms, separating them. Actually, there were two different bedspreads, each nailed to the ceiling. When a person went between the rooms he parted them in the middle and stepped through, using them the same way you would a sliding door.

"Here, honey," Tina said, holding out a book of matches she had extracted from her purse.

As Jo-Jo leaned over to get the matches his eyes fell on the roll of money in her purse. "Damn, but that seems like a lot of money," he stated, nodding at her open purse.

"Yeah, I know what you mean. It's all those one-dollar bills we took in. Shit, Jo-Jo, we musta taken in over two hundred dollars in singles alone." She smiled suddenly and the smile made the light-complexioned woman look much younger than her twenty-five years. When she smiled the hard lines around her mouth disappeared. Tall, thin, and gaunt to the extent that she appeared to be undernourished, she still retained a small amount of attractiveness.

On the other hand, when Jo-Jo opened his mouth it took something from him. His teeth were rotten, typical of the person who has used hard narcotics for ten years or better. It was catching up with him. He was as slim as his woman.

"Naw, baby, I don't think we'll have the delay we had the last time. Remember on the last cop we were short on the man's money, so I think he did it more or less to teach us a lesson." As he talked, Jo-Jo tore four matches from the book and struck them. He held the burning matches under the cooker until the matches almost burned his fingers. Then he shook the matches out before casually dropping them on the floor.

"Shit! If you had to do the cleaning up, Jo-Jo, you wouldn't be so quick to throw everything you finish with on the damn floor!"

Jo-Jo laughed sharply as he set the hot cooker down on the edge of the coffee table in front of him. His reddish brown eyes surveyed the cluttered floor. There was such an accumulation of trash that it appeared as if no one had bothered to sweep up in over a month. The short brown-skinned man grinned up at his woman. "It don't look as if you been killin' yourself cleaning up."

"Shit!" she snorted again. "If it wasn't for them nasty-ass friends of yours, the place would be clean."

"I'll sweep up for you, Momma," a young voice called out from the dining room-bedroom.

Before either of the grownups could say no, the six-year-old child appeared, pulling a broom along that was taller than she was. Little Tina was a smaller model of her mother, light-complexioned, with dimples in each cheek. She smiled brightly at her mother and stepfather as she tried to make herself helpful.

The appearance of the child didn't stop Jo-Jo in his preparation of the drugs. He removed a stocking from a small brown paper bag, then an eyedropper that had two needles stuck in the bulb part of the dropper. Jo-Jo removed both the needles, then inserted one of them on the end of the dropper.

"Leave me enough to draw up, Jo-Jo," Tina begged before he had even drawn up a drop.

He smiled up at her encouragingly, "Don't worry, honey, don't I always look out for my baby?"

"You can get right funky, Jo-Jo, when the last of the junk is in sight. You're real cool when there's a lot of the jive, but you get doggish as a mother-fucker when it ain't but a little bit left."

Unknown to the couple, little Tina had moved closer to the table, swinging the broom back and forth vigorously.

Tina opened up the paper bag and removed another dropper from it. "Is that other spike any good?" she asked anxiously.

"How the fuck would I know?" he cursed sharply as he attempted to open up the needle on his dropper. "This motherfucker of mine is stopped up!"

"No wonder," Tina said as she attempted to draw up some water from the dirty glass that Jo-Jo was using.

"Your glass has got so much filth in it, it's a wonder you ain't ruined the dope in the cooker." She glanced over his shoulder at the cooker. "You used that water in the glass, didn't you?"

Jo-Jo shrugged. "It don't make no difference, once I put the fire under it. It killed any germs that might have been in the motherfuckin' water."

"Yeah," she answered worriedly, "you may have killed the so-called germs, but what about all that trash we got to draw up?"

In exasperation Jo-Jo cursed, "I don't know what the fuck you want me to do about it. It's done, ain't nothing else I can do. If you're really that motherfuckin' worried over it, Tina, take your ass out to the kitchen and get some more clean water."

"Shit!" she exclaimed, using her stock phrase.

"By the time I got back, you'd be done drawin' up all the dope and shot it."

"Goddamn, woman, you don't trust nobody, do you?"

"Daddy, I'll go get you some more water," Little Tina said as she rushed over to the table in an attempt to be helpful. The tall broom she carried was too much for her to control completely. As she neared the table, dragging the broom, the handle swung down in an arc.

Too late, Jo-Jo threw his hand up as if to ward off a blow. The handle came down and struck the cooker, sending it spinning off the end of the table. The drug in the bottom of it spilled out as the top fell off the end of the table onto the dirty throw rug. Instantly the rug absorbed the drug so that it was impossible for the two addicts to save any of it.

Tina dropped down on her knees beside the table. She picked up the overturned cooker. "It wasn't any cotton in the cooker," she stated in a hurt voice. She turned it around and around, as if she couldn't believe it had happened. Suddenly she started to paw at the rug, rubbing it as she searched for some of the liquid that had escaped.

"Not a fuckin' drop left!" she managed to say. "The goddamn rug was like a fuckin' sponge!"

The little girl backed away from the table. Her mouth was open as she pleaded, "I didn't mean it, I'm sorry." Tears ran down both her cheeks.

Instantly Jo-Jo exploded as the sound of her

voice brought him out of his trance. He snatched the broom from the child's hand and began beating her about the head with it. With one vicious blow, he broke the broom in half across the child's head.

The little girl attempted to cover up, but it didn't do any good. Jo-Jo snatched her hands down from in front of her face and began to beat her in the face with his fists. He rained blow after blow on the child's exposed face until blood ran from her nose and mouth. When Little Tina fell down at his feet, Jo-Jo drew his foot back and began to kick her viciously in the side.

"You little bitch," he screamed in rage. "God damn you, I done told you to stay the fuck out of the way when I'm makin' up." He grew more angry as he cursed and, instead of the sight of the bleeding child at his feet drawing pity, it only aroused his anger.

Suddenly he reached down and snatched the child to her feet. Her feeble cry of pain only enraged him. "You bitch," he swore over and over, "I'm going to fix your little meddling ass once and for all!"

In pure terror, the girl managed to break away. She ran back towards the bedroom and attempted to hide under the bed.

Jo-Jo followed closely behind her. He drew his heavy leather belt from off his pants and, grabbing the child's leg, he pulled her from under the bed.

Her screams rang out clear and loud as the belt

CRIME PARTNERS

began to fall, slowly at first and then faster. She squirmed and tried to crawl away from the pain that exploded all over her body. Sometimes the fire would explode on her back, then around her tender legs, but what hurt her the most was when it wrapped around her and the metal part of the belt would dig into her stomach and hips.

"Jo-Jo, Jo-Jo, what you trying to do?" Tina screamed, holding the dividing curtains apart. "If you kill that child, it ain't goin' bring the dope back."

It took a moment for her words to penetrate the blind rage that engulfed him. For a few seconds he couldn't see or think right, but as his senses returned and he saw the bloody child lying on the floor, his anger fled and fear shot through him. Why was she lying so still?

"Tina, Little Tina, get your ass up from there and go in the toilet and wash up," he ordered harshly. He waited impatiently for the child to jump up and obey his order. "Get up," he screamed, his voice breaking slightly. He took his foot and kicked her. "I said get up."

"Don't kick my child," the mother yelled as she came closer. "I done warned you about whipping her so hard, Jo-Jo. If we have to take her to the hospital, I ain't takin' no blame for all those marks on her."

"We ain't going to no hospital," Jo-Jo stated coldly. "All this bitch has got to do is get up and go in the bathroom and wash up. Get up, Tina, I ain't mad no more. I'll get some more stuff later on, don't worry about it," he yelled down at her before kneeling beside her. He put his arms under the frail child's neck and legs, lifted her slowly, and then placed her gently on the bed. He didn't know that it was too late for gentleness now.

"She looks like she's turning blue," Tina screamed out. She frantically clutched at the child. "What's wrong with her? Why is she laying so still? Tina, Tina, wake up, girl!"

The mother's fear quickly transferred to the waiting man. Jo-Jo could feel the knot of fear growing in the pit of his stomach. The child couldn't be dead; that he was sure of. He hadn't hit her hard enough for that. No way, he told himself in an attempt to quiet his jumping nerves.

"Oh, Jo-Jo, you got to do something. Man, what's wrong with my little girl? Please, Jo-Jo, do something for her."

If there had been anything he could have done, Jo-Jo would have done it. But he didn't know what to do. All he could do was stare down at the unconscious form and somewhere in the back of his mind he realized what he was too frightened to face. The child was dead. He knew it yet wouldn't face up to the fact.

Little Tina had received her last beating. There would be no more sleepless nights for the child because she was too hungry to sleep. No more lying awake, hoping her mother would come out of her nod long enough to get up and cook something. There would be no more fears of uncontrolled beatings, beatings that came for nothing. Yes, Little Tina was beyond that—beyond a mother's love that sometimes seemed more like hate.

1

THE TWO DETECTIVES had been sitting in their office at the downtown police precinct since early morning, waiting for one phone call. When the telephone finally rang, both men leaped to their feet. The black officer beat his white partner to the phone. He winked at his friend, letting him know that this was the call they had been waiting for.

The tall, chisel-faced white man walked back to his old beat-up desk and sat down. Detective Ryan drummed his fingers on the top of the well-scarred desk as he waited impatiently for the call to come to an end.

Finally the tall black man hung up the phone. "Well, what the hell are you going to do," he yelled over to his partner as Ryan jumped to his feet, "sit there on your dead ass all day?"

"Screw you, Benson, you cocksucker you," Ryan yelled back as both men moved hurriedly towards the door. "Did the informer give up all the information we need?"

Detective Edward Benson slowed down enough to show Ryan a piece of paper on which he had hurriedly written down an address. "We've got the bastard's address, just like he said he'd get."

The two men walked hurriedly down a short corridor that led into an outer office. The detectives threaded their way through the cluttered office, greeting the men and women over the hum of the old-fashioned air conditioner.

As the black and white detectives neared the outer door, two younger detectives sitting nearby came to their feet. Neither man appeared to be over twenty-five years old, while Benson and Ryan both had wrinkles under their eyes that were not there from lack of sleep. Both of the older detectives appeared to be in their late thirties or early forties. They were replicas of what the younger men would look like in ten years if they stayed on their jobs as crime fighters. The work would take its toll.

The two young white detectives ignored Benson and spoke to his partner. It was done more out of habit than to slight Benson deliberately. "We were told to wait for you, sir, that you might need backup men," the taller of the two said.

Ryan stopped and stared at the men. He hadn't missed the slur to his black partner. "I don't know,"

Ryan answered harshly. "It's up to my senior officer, Detective Benson." He nodded in the direction of the black officer.

The two young white detectives glanced down at the floor in embarrassment. Neither man wanted to come out and ask Benson directly if they could go along, but it would be a good point on their record if they could be in on the arrest of two murderers.

"What do you think, Ben?" Ryan asked his partner, breaking the silence.

Benson glanced coldly at the two younger officers. "It's up to you, Ryan, if you think you might need some help arresting the punks." He shrugged his shoulders, showing by his actions that he really didn't want the men along.

Ryan knew what the problem was. If the men had spoken to Benson when they first walked up, he would have taken them along gladly. But now he didn't want to be bothered with them. It was written all over his face. In the years Ryan had worked with him, he had come to find that the intelligent black man was extremely sensitive. At times, it seemed as if he was too sensitive. Ryan started to tell the young men to come along anyway but changed his mind. There was no sense in antagonizing the man he had to work with.

As Benson went out the door, Ryan turned to the two men sheepishly. "Well, I guess there won't be any need for your help after all. It shouldn't take four of us to bring in two punks."

It was apparent that the two men were disappointed. One of them started to say something but decided against it. Their brief exchange hadn't gone unnoticed by some of the other officers in the department. Most of them had been aware of what the men had been waiting for. As Ryan went out the door, leaving the men behind, the workers in the office glanced down, not wanting to catch the eyes of the rejected men.

Ryan caught up with his partner in the garage underneath the station. This was where they brought their prisoners. They took them out of the cars, still handcuffed, and led them to the three elevators that were located in the center of the garage. No matter where a policeman parked, he didn't have far to go to transport his prisoner. There were two uniformed policemen stationed in the garage at all times to help, if help was ever needed. The garage was also a good place for the policemen to kick the shit out of their prisoners, out of sight of any watching eyes. The garage detail never went against another officer, no matter how brutally policeman might treat a handcuffed prisoner.

"You could have brought those guys along, Ryan," Benson said, drumming his fingers impatiently on the steering wheel.

Ryan shook his head as Benson drove out of the garage. "Naw, Ben, it's like you said; what the hell do we need with help? It ain't but two punks that we're after."

Benson knew Ryan was lying, as well as he knew

he had been wrong in rejecting the help of the fellow officers. They were on their way to arrest Billy Good and his crime partner, Jackie Walker. Both men were believed to be professional killers. In such a case, there should be backup men on the job. If something should happen to Ryan because of Benson's anger, he would never get over it. But as he picked up the two-way radio and put in a call, giving the address they were headed for and requesting the support of a black-and-white car, Benson got a feeling of satisfaction. He knew that the two younger detectives would hear about it and know they had been rejected while two uniformed men had been called in to do what they had been refused the honor of doing.

Ryan only glanced straight ahead. He knew what his partner had done and realized that it was another blow to the pride of the younger officers. As it was, Benson wasn't the most liked officer in the homicide division. And after this got out, which it would, he would be liked even less.

"You think these guys will give us any trouble?" Ryan asked as they left the freeway at Clay Avenue and made a left turn.

Benson gave his standard shrug. "I haven't thought about it one way or the other. I could care less either way," he answered coldly.

Even as the policemen got off the freeway eight blocks from their destination, events were taking place that would change their lives.

Billy Good was parking the car in front of his

and Jackie's apartment. Jackie kissed his girlfriend, Carol, one more time before getting out. They had just come from Kenyatta's farm, where they had been staying for the past week. Ever since making the hit on Kingfisher's dope pusher, Little David, they'd been out of town.

Billy, who had driven the whole way back from the farm, stretched his arms out, then caressed Joy's neck. The tall, black beauty riding next to him smiled contentedly. Joy had finally found a man she could really love. This short, husky, brown-skinned man wasn't what she'd dreamed her lover man would look like, but he'd proven he was more than adequate. She had no apprehensions when she was with him, It was a new and gratifying experience for her.

The men she'd had in the past had always depended on her, mostly for an income. Now she had a man who wasn't concerned with how much money she could make. He just wanted her for herself.

This was the first time Joy had ever been to the apartment that Billy shared with Jackie. She had just met Billy when Kenyatta brought him and Jackie out to the farm and had given a party in their honor. She smiled to herself smugly as she remembered that first night in Billy's arms. What a night it had been! They'd made love until dawn, and then she couldn't really sleep, afraid that when she awoke it would all have been a dream.

Carol and Jackie got out of the car first and

waited on the pavement for Billy to come around the car and join them. They made a curious couple, him being over six foot five while she was only five foot.

Billy came around the car grinning. Neither of the two couples paid much attention to the well-dressed black men who got out of the black Cadillac down the street and hurried toward them. The first warning came when the men had gotten close and Jackie noticed one of them open up his suitcoat and take out what looked like a short iron pipe. Before he could react, he realized that it was a sawed-off shotgun.

He screamed out in panic. "Watch out, Billy, they got shotguns!"

The sound of his voice hadn't died out before the afternoon quiet was shattered by the sound of shotguns going off.

Joy had been admiring the new home she was going to move into when she was struck down. Half of her neck was blown off. Billy was spattered with the blood of his loved one. He screamed—a dying scream full of hate and frustration as he made a frantic move for his shoulder holster. Unknown strength kept him on his feet as the first shotgun shells hit him high in the chest. He fell back against the car, somehow managing to remove the gun from its place of concealment. But it was no use. He died with the weapon still in his hand.

Carol's screams shattered the stillness as she

DEATH LIST

watched Jackie topple over, his tall frame crumbling as he kept falling until the hard pavement struck him in the face. Her screams were cut off abruptly as half her mouth and face were blown away. She was dead before she hit the cold ground.

Black faces peered out of the windows of the nearby buildings, but no one came to the rescue of the stricken couples. Blood ran freely down off the sidewalk into the gutter as the lifeless forms of four young black people lay in the filth and hopelessness of the hard-pressed neighborhood.

Down the street, the long black Cadillac moved away from the curb, filled with black men who made killing their business. Even as Detectives Benson and Ryan turned onto the street, the black car disappeared around the corner.

Benson slammed on his brakes next to the murder scene. The black-and-white backup car came from the opposite end of the street, having turned the same corner that the black Cadillac had.

Benson walked from one body to the next, examining the dead. When he reached Jackie's long body, he thought he heard a moan, but there was so much blood he believed it must be his imagination. He bent down and lifted up the bloody head, cradling Jackie in his arms as if he were a loved one.

"I think this one is still with us," he yelled out as Ryan came over.

Ryan flinched at the sight. He had seen many murders before, but whenever he came upon a shotgun killing, it was always horrible. This one was even worse than most. It was the first time he'd ever seen women shot down in such a vicious manner.

Ryan stood over his partner and called out to one of the uniformed officers who was running over with a gun in his hand. "Call for an ambulance," he ordered sharply, his voice cracking with emotion.

As Ryan glanced around at the other uniformed policeman, he saw the young black officer bent over by the car, throwing up his afternoon meal. The sight of the man puking almost made Ryan do the same thing.

Benson stood up. "He can change that call; we don't need an ambulance. What we need is a meat wagon." He walked away, unaware of the blood that was on his new blue suit.